To all my readers who have no shelf control and picked up this series even though you're in the middle of three others, this book is for you <3

AN ENDING THAT'LL HAVE YOU IN KNOTS...

My enemy isn't who I thought it was.

My Alphas have groveled, begged, and fallen to their knees to plead for my forgiveness.

I'm still not sure I'm ready, but I'll need to find a way if I want to face what's coming next.

The Hunters and the packs are stuck in a stalemate while some invisible force plucks us off one-by-one.

The Storms have gone out of control and continue to destroy the forest, the leaves, and any life it touches.

And when I go home, even my own family turns their backs on me.

It doesn't matter that I've saved my sister—I'm one of the wolves to her now.

I'm an Outcast and I know what Kane has felt for the first time.

I need to find a way to forgive my alphas.

Because if I can't… how can I expect my family to find a way to forgive *me*?

THE STORY SO FAR...

Katlyn

Book One Recap

I'm just a regular human trying to survive at the edge of the world. The wolves only know how to take.

They take our land.

They take our lives.

They take our will to survive.

Ever since they gained in power and settled into Crescent City, the storms began. My sister and I were caught in one a few years back.

Her faded eyes still haunt me and drive me to ensure no one else is taken from me.

That no one else has to suffer an existence like this.

The Moon Shadow Plague has destroyed too many lives already.

My older sister who won't be named.

Charlie's father.

I won't let them take my sister Luna from me, too.

So that's why I went out there with Charlie to collect what Moon Blossoms were left. The magical blooms are the only things that can shield a home from the offensive magic.

And when it's the High Moon Ceremony, there's a shit ton of it to go around.

I could smell the metallic hint of the storms in the air. The only problem was that the storms were three days early.

Charlie didn't understand the seriousness of the situation. He's not like me. He hadn't undergone a mysterious change.

And I couldn't tell him that I'm different.

It might just be more than a heightened sense of smell. What if something else was wrong with me?

He still had hope, although I have no idea where he gets it from.

And I didn't want to take that from him. His hope was something I cling to, as well.

When he began a game of moon tag, he expected me to track him.

A game to cheer me up on what would become the worst day of my life.

That's how I like to remember Charlie.

The fine layer of dirt caking our bodies wasn't enough to cloak us from any stray wolves. We'd never gone that far north before, but with the scarcity of the Moon Blossoms there wasn't much choice.

It didn't end well for Charlie. A wolf found him.

Although I still don't know which one.

Charlie could have run. The selfless idiot ate a Moon Blossom instead, turning himself into a beacon to buy me time to escape.

He should have known me better than that.

Even though I let my arrow fly, it wasn't enough.

He's dead. The wolves have taken him from me.

I'm broken.

No… not broken.

Enraged.

The hope he carried had been decimated. As did all the Moon Blossoms he had gathered.

With the icy rain already falling and stinging my cheeks, I was faced with an impossible choice.

I couldn't go home empty-handed, and I didn't have time to find more of the Moon Blossoms.

I had to go into the city.

There, I would stop the ceremony… and I would stop the storms.

I needed to end this once and for all.

When I ventured into the city, I came across dead bodies.

Someone might be helping me. I don't know why, but I also don't care.

All that matters is protecting what family I have left. If someone wants to kill off some wolves for me, they can be my guest.

When I reached the Epicenter, I found the ceremony in full force. The wolves underestimated me. They saw me just as a human who had borrowed a little bit of their magic.

I'm so much more than that.

I'm a woman scorned and their death is a sweet taste I crave in my mouth.

There were three alphas on the moondial as the ceremony went into effect. Their Goddess is going to descend and the hum of magic in the air sent all my hairs on end.

A fourth alpha dragged me to the dial before I could do more damage. The others wisely encouraged him to kill me, but something strange had happened between all of us.

I wanted to scratch… bite… and draw blood.

I didn't know at the time that biting my captor would initiate a mating bond.

That sensation I had that something was different about me since my exposure to the storms was starting to make sense.

I was absorbing their magic… not rejecting it like a human should.

And when the Moon Crescent descended from the heavens, I gathered every bit of the magic I had absorbed to launch myself high enough to take it into my tiny grip.

All the alphas tried to stop me, resulting in every single alpha of the four packs placing their hands on me during a critical moment.

When I crushed the heart of their Goddess, it didn't destroy her.

It sent her soul into me.

The resulting shockwave of magic mated me to the alpha of every pack.

They couldn't accept such blasphemy.

They rejected me.

One by one they announced their refusal.

It hurt.

Oh gods, it hurt.

Their wolves didn't approve, but their human minds secured the decision before their shift began.

And I ran.

The ceremony called for the chase. I didn't know at the time that the wolves would be deep in the rut by the time they found me.

They would bite, but with the human order, they would bite a little too hard.

It wouldn't take much to snap a human's neck.

Except, I wasn't quite human anymore. Something new and ancient at the same time had awakened deep within me.

My wolf.

And she told me that only one wolf could successfully reject me by my death. The rest would live on in suffering, unable to mate or procreate, unable to do anything but exist.

It gave me a dark moment of hesitation, but I couldn't end my life just for the satisfaction of knowing they would all suffer. There could be other packs I didn't know about, and wouldn't there just be new alphas to take their place?

I decided to run. And when I was cornered in a tree while the other alphas fought over the right to kill me, a female white wolf helped me escape.

Her name is Althea and she's a magical wolf. She told me of her visions and of prophecies.

I thought she was a little off her nut at first, but she

proved that her words were true when she took me to a hidden mansion deep within the wolves' territory.

She says I'm the Moon Guardian.

That the storms existed to find me... a human vessel for their Goddess to be reborn and to unite the packs.

Not four packs... but five.

When I met their alpha, it changed everything.

Kane.

He is *perfect*. He offered his life up to me willingly and made me wonder if I've had this all wrong.

Perhaps the wolves aren't my enemy, or maybe they still are.

Everything is muddled and confused when I'm with him. And when our courtship begins, I'm pushed into heat.

The alphas are outside the mansion howling for me, demanding to be let in.

I'm trapped and my soul is screaming for reprieve.

The High Moon has passed, so I cannot be claimed. We all must suffer, but where is there to go?

What will happen when they find me?

All of my human concerns become a distant memory when my bones begin to break.

And my first shift begins.

Book Two Recap

Everything changes when I accept my wolf.

What surprises me most is that she's always been with me. She's not a new creation—she's a part of me that's been awakened.

Which means I have questions.

Questions that won't have answers, not when I'm in the throes of my first heat.

My alphas have called me, and it is their demanding cries that rip my wolf out from my soul and bring her to the forefront.

It didn't help that Kane had been awakening my desire just as much as my wolf. He introduced me to the way he worships, which means using his tongue.

In a very unholy way.

I began a courtship with him that seems right, but I'm betrayed when he orders Althea and a sheepish girl by the name of Nina to "restrain me."

Then he's gone, leaving me to be dragged into a cave and chained like a wild animal.

I discover that Nina is part "Hunter," a species that even the wolves fear.

And if the wolves fear something, I'm not sure how I'm supposed to stand a chance.

This appears to be the true division between the five packs. The Moon Pack, now called the Outcasts, have Hunter blood in their ranks.

And those Hunters have descended on our realm looking for *me*.

I never asked for any of this. I'm just trying to survive.

And process the death of my best friend, Charlie.

And hope that my family made it through the storms.

Meanwhile, my wolf is trying to break free and rip through my body.

Breaking every bone.

Reforming every tendon.

And the process finally renders me unconscious after such overwhelming pain.

When I wake, I find myself bound by magical chains.

And I'm on all fours covered in fur, and very much a wolf.

The alphas who rejected me are chained as well and Kane is here, coaxing me, apologizing, and injured.

Because he single-handedly fought off a group of Hunters who came for me as well as the alphas of the other four packs.

He's so powerful.

And now, it's time to take that strength for myself.

The Goddess inside of me has grown along with my wolf. It's so natural to tap into both of them and utilize their gifts.

I'm a trinity in a small package.

I decide to forgive Kane. He was trying to protect me and didn't want me to run out of fear, landing right into a group of Hunters intent on killing me.

That's why he chained me, and now, he's set me free.

He wants me to reject them, but I want them to suffer more than that.

Rejection is easy. I already know what that feels like and they deserve something worse.

Like watching Kane Claim me right in front of them.

There's one problem. That requires the power of the High Moon which only comes once every lunar cycle.

It's a good thing I'm the Moon Guardian.

Determined to show the strength of my will, I bring the High Moon down on us, even in a cave, even though it's not time.

I'm a Goddess, after all.

When Kane Claims me in my human form, it's absolutely *incredible*.

While the alphas watching are jealous, they're just as enraptured as I am.

And while I'm supposed to reject them, our connection seems to strengthen instead.

Althea said that my fate was to unite the five packs, and my wolf seems intent on accomplishing that task the only way she knows how. By taking control of the situation as Queen.

It puts me in a precarious position.

Because just a few moments ago, I was plotting their deaths.

Before I have a chance to decide what to do, a Hunter has shown up and turned himself in.

Kane underestimates him. While he's restrained and surrounded by the entirety of the Moon Pack, he's come with a plan in place.

One that he enacts the moment he sees me, taking me through a portal to a horrible place where the moon refuses to shine.

After attempting to stab me in the heart.

Wounded, scared, and alone, I suffer in silence as the Hunter deprives me of food and water.

For a month.

I'm convinced that I'm going to die until the Goddess

herself appears to me. She explains that we've been taken to Hell's Heart—which makes sense. This place is hot and horrible.

But soon, the High Moon will make its appearance along with my alphas.

It's my chance for an escape. I don't question how the realms have found a way to merge. Or how my alphas have found a way to work together to find me.

I go to them and I take my chance to escape the heat and the hunger.

Now I'm back in the forest on all fours, embracing my wolf like I should have the first time the High Moon had appeared.

This is my second chance.

One I won't squander.

So now it's time to *run*.

KATLYN

Run, little moon.

Run like the wind.

And if you're good, I'm going to catch you and make you scream.

Kane's voice echoed in my mind as I ran with all my might.

The thrill of his promise made me pant with excitement, but there was a process to this courtship.

Run.

Play.

Claim.

But first, I needed to prepare. I'd been starved and deprived of food and drink for an entire month—something I wouldn't have survived without the power of the Goddess strong in my veins.

Energy that had been denied to me for an entire month swept back into my body in massive waves.

My *wolf's* body.

It felt so good to be powerful, fast, and unstoppable.

The world flashed around me in a blur as I let my primal spirit take over. Her guidance set my paws in the right places. It didn't matter that she'd never had the chance to run like this before—the Goddess knew what to do.

And she gave us wisdom beyond our years, remedying all of the experiences that had been denied to us through a natural instinct that made everything feel surreal.

It was as if I'd always run as a wolf under the High Moon.

Because I knew what to do. My alphas were on my tail, but couldn't keep up.

I knew they were trying. Their growls sent ripples over my fur. I didn't have to speak their language to know they were demanding for me to submit and return to my human form so that I could take their knots.

A deep ache beckoned me to give them what they wanted. If I shifted back into my human form, I would feel the full effect of my heat.

Which was precisely why I stayed in wolf form. My alphas could still smell me, and I had no doubt it was driving them mad, but I could remain in control.

My instincts also told me that submitting wouldn't befit our status as the Omega Goddess.

We needed to see who was worthy, which meant a test was in order.

When my alphas found me, there would be blood.

And then there would be a true Claiming. While Kane had already Claimed me, the others had thrown away their chance.

And I wasn't so sure if I was ready to give them another one. It depended on what happened next.

Although, a fight for the right to Claim would be a good start.

While it would be fun to witness the brutality that would determine who would knot me first, I knew that I wouldn't be of use to anyone without initially finding something to empower me more than simply the light of the High Moon.

My body was still physical. It had tested the limits of my Goddess's spirit to keep me alive. Before embracing my full potential, I needed to take care of my basic needs.

My wolf whined at me with that train of thought. There were five alphas who definitely wanted to see to my *needs*, but that particular need was going to have to wait.

She was lost to the heat, but I wasn't. Not until I was ready.

I darted past towering trees beneath a bright High Moon. My paws thudded against the soft ground and the night air beckoned me with its crisp embrace.

It was such a nice reprieve after the horrid dry heat of the past month.

It wasn't just the break from the heat that soothed my soul, but the contrast between life and death.

Hell's Heart had been an empty void with no one to converse with and nothing to hold onto.

Here, everything had a voice and a spirit.

Glimpses between full trees allowed me to see bright stars that twinkled, as if they too were celebrating my return.

The entire forest was alive.

Foxes, rabbits, stags, and birds of all shapes and sizes

fluttered from my path. They chirped, squeaked, and called to me with various languages I didn't yet understand.

I was the Queen of the night and the heart of this forest.

It existed to serve me, and I existed to cultivate it in return.

The spirit of the Goddess was one of life, not death. She disapproved of the slaughter of so many humans, which was why she had sided with the Moon Pack during the war.

Yet something had been draining her power.

Or someone.

That train of thought was cut off when the scent of wet moss hit my nose.

A creek.

My wolf stirred in approval as I ran toward the music of rushing water. I navigated the challenging twists and turns through thick brush and well-hidden glimmers of iron.

Traps, I realized. The Goddess within me had been guiding me to avoid them.

Faint concern filtered into my mind at leading my alphas into danger, but my wolf immediately calmed my fears.

If they cannot follow you, they are not worthy of you.

That was true. Part of the chase included a challenge. Tonight was a second chance at the mating ceremony as it should have been.

They had to earn me. And after everything that had happened, I wouldn't make it easy for them.

They might have allowed me to escape Hell's Heart, but that wasn't enough. If I was going to embrace this life as a wolf, then I had to be sure the alphas at my side could handle any danger I might find myself in.

So I deftly launched left, then right, and bounded over a series of complex traps.

They were old, but evidence of an earlier war with the Hunters that I had only heard about in legend. The wolves had once faced an enemy that threatened their existence. Still, I had always written those stories off as fantastical dreams.

Plus, if the Hunters were so frightening, how did they lose?

The question nagged at me as I navigated the old traps using instincts supplied by the Goddess. My snout led me, my nostrils flaring when I picked up the old hint of iron and danger.

I'd been held captive by a single Hunter in another realm for an entire month.

Yet, he hadn't been able to kill me.

That said something of the power of the Moon Goddess, didn't it?

Maybe it was the Goddess who had driven them off.

If so, why hadn't she protected the humans as well?

Because I was too weak, my dear, a voice lingered in my mind. Just like my wolf, her voice was mine, but not mine at the same time. The similar tones rang with hints of bells and a whisper of wind in the trees.

A swirl of emotions squeezed my strong wolf's heart. The Goddess had aligned with the Moon Pack for a reason. They valued all life, as did she.

She wanted humanity to live and thrive. I couldn't deny that need that burned in my chest that resonated with all three parts of my trinity spirit.

Yet, didn't Althea say that the storms had been created to find me? Wouldn't the Goddess know that would all but push humanity to extinction?

The storms themselves do not injure life, my kindred spirit. It is the Corruption that has done this.

It is Corruption that must be defeated. And only with the united might of all five clans I have created can we hope to stand up to the Conduit.

None of what the Goddess was telling me made any sense.

Corruption?

Conduit?

These terms were starting to get on my nerves the more I heard them.

My wolf entirely agreed. War and schemes were things of men, and right now, she would focus on a wolf's needs.

My throat was dry and cracked, as were my paws. We needed water. We needed food.

We needed more moonlight.

The distant call of nature's music enticed me, signaling we had arrived at the water's edge.

The Goddess inside of me retreated, agreeing with the wolf. I broke through the final layers of foliage to find our prize.

And I wasted no time splashing into the water.

Elation swept through me when I stepped into the rocky bed of a running creek. The water cooled our paws and seemed to revitalize my spirit simply by washing my fur.

I realized it was because the water had absorbed the moonlight, which gave me power that had been sorely drained.

I paused to admire the scene as the High Moon broke through the clearing, sending the water glittering like diamonds encased in glass.

Moon Blossoms dotted the bank and added a diamond gleam to the atmosphere.

It was clear that this place had remained untouched for years—the moss around the banks running unfettered. The perimeter was untainted by human feet or wolf claws.

The untouched quality allowed all life to glow with the silver caress of the High Moon.

We feast, my wolf said with pure joy.

I agreed.

First I sank my snout into the water and lapped it up. If I had been human, I would have groaned at how good it felt to have the cool water tickling down my throat.

My wolf guided me to the real feast waiting in the water. Glimmers of silver betrayed the presence of fish.

They were unlike any fish I had ever seen—not that I'd seen many. Most of the creek beds had been affected by the Moon Shadow Plague near my village, so fish had become something of a delicacy.

The few tiny minnows I'd eaten before were nothing like these massive creatures that flitted under the glassy waters. I stared at them, mesmerized by their strength and size as they overturned smaller rocks on the creek's bed. Some swallowed them whole, then spit them out.

That one, my wolf decided, literally salivating as she homed in on the largest of the fish.

I dove, all teeth and claws as I sank my snout into the water and locked my jaw around it.

Its flesh gave underneath my bite and a sense of victory shot through me. My wolf was in control, overriding any hesitation I might have had as she deftly snapped the fish's spine.

A quick death. She didn't enjoy killing. We were a trinity of life, the Goddess, my wolf and I—but wolves fed on meat.

And so we devoured the sacrifice the moonlit creek offered—scales and bones whole.

I let my wolf's spirit take over as she hunted three more of the massive fish.

As I took my fill, my human mind drifted back to thoughts of my alphas.

Had they followed my trail? Shouldn't they be here by now?

Worry tugged at my stomach. Mostly for Kane, but I knew that the other alphas had a purpose, too.

My goal was to save my village and restore humanity —which meant putting Kane back into a place of power. Mating the alphas of all his rival packs would give him a measure of control that I could only imagine he'd never had before.

He'd lost a war against them once. Brute force clearly didn't work.

The Goddess inside of me was on my side. She wanted humanity to live, and she had a plan to accomplish it.

One that would be ruined if they failed to navigate the old traps that led to this place. Some hadn't been visible at all. The provided memories from the Goddess allowed me to know where all of them had been buried.

They're strong, my wolf assured me. *They'll prove to be worthy.*

Finishing off the last of the fish, my strength slowly returned.

With renewed energy, I made my way up the creek bed, following the sound of rushing water. It seemed to beckon me forward toward a precipice in the stone.

Once I crested a series of large rocks, I easily bounded to the top and took in a large clearing.

A knot worked itself in my throat when I recognized a campsite with unmistakable fires and tents. A particularly large structure had been erected between two ancient sequoias.

My wolf's sight was superior in many ways, but she was rather near-sighted.

So instead, I relied on my nose to tell me what was below—and how many.

The first scent overpowered the others—one of old blood and dark magic.

Hunters, my wolf hissed in my mind as a growl rumbled in my throat.

My hackles rose as I tried to make out the weaker scent.

This one was more familiar, one that I had recognized from my village. It consisted of sweat, ash, and crusty dried bread that many of my people lived off of in-between fresh game.

Humans.

Which meant that members of my village were here farther north than any of them had ever traveled before, and they were with the Hunters.

What the hell is going on?

I didn't have time to ponder the question because the wind shifted, dousing me with an overpowering third scent.

Alphas.

Hundreds of them.

RYKER

"Ow, fuck!" I shouted as I stubbed my toe on yet another fucking rock.

This is bullshit.

A pathetically human growl rumbled in my throat as I slowly worked my way through the forest.

I had never felt more mortal in all my life.

So weak, blind, and fragile.

All because my wolf had abandoned me and still hadn't returned.

"You expect me to track her as a human?" I snarled at the silent wolf inside my soul. I ripped away another branch that had gotten in my way, only to hiss when the thorns ripped my skin.

I'd never experienced this. My wolf and I had always been one, but right now he had left me to my fate. The result was me floundering through the moonlit woods barely able to see and subjected to every little rock and branch damaging my skin.

Was it like this for all humans? Because this sucked.

No wonder they didn't walk around naked like shifters. Even the tiniest weed dug itself into my ankle and forced me to stop to pluck it out, leaving behind a wound.

Where was my damn wolf?

His last words rang in my mind on an eternal loop.

You rejected her.

You lost *her.*

Now you find her and fix this.

My animal thought that this was all my fault.

She was human, or at least, she had been when I'd first found her.

She wasn't human. You just failed to recognize what I saw. You failed to listen.

My wolf wasn't talking to me, but I knew him well enough to imagine what he might say.

I wasn't supposed to override my wolf except in exceptional circumstances. I'd rarely had to, but we were supposed to be the alpha of our pack. It was up to me to make sure we didn't fuck it up.

Everything hinged on unwavering loyalty to the Goddess when it came to being an alpha of the Mercury Pack.

And by unwavering, that meant complete, utter reverence to the deity that had created us.

To the point that I hadn't even taken a female. Unlike the other alphas, I demonstrated my control and strength by ignoring my wolf's aggressive sexual needs. A vow of celibacy had ruled my basic instincts all my life and was only one facet of my service to the Goddess.

When I took a mate, I would unleash all of that pent-up energy.

A human couldn't handle that, much less survive it.

Even if she didn't deserve to be rejected, it was imperative that my mate help me grow as an alpha, not drag me down.

And what kind of servant to my Goddess would I be if I mated the very human who destroyed Her heart right in front of me?

Except, she hadn't destroyed my Goddess. That's what my wolf had been trying to tell me from the very beginning.

She was the Moon Guardian. She was a *legend*.

Cursing myself for not seeing it earlier, I begrudgingly accepted my punishment of stumbling through the forest.

Honestly, I deserved worse.

Pausing, I knelt to get a better view of some broken branches. Something white glinted with the silver of the moon and caught my attention, even with my annoyingly weak human vision.

Rubbing the fluff between my fingers, my heart stuttered with excitement.

Because, by some miracle, I was still on her trail.

I'd reach her much later than the others, which put me at a disadvantage, but giving up wasn't in my nature.

"I'll find you, pup," I said under my breath as I continued down the path she'd gone.

While she'd done a good job hiding her steps, the alphas who followed her made no effort to work under stealth.

Both of those realizations interested me.

The first was unusual, given that the Moon Guardian had never run as her wolf before. It was a testament to what and who she was. She held the spirit of the Moon Goddess within her, and I should be on my hands and knees before her praising her name.

That required finding her, first.

Which made the second point quite fascinating. The alphas who followed her were experienced wolves. They knew how to hide their heavy tracks, but they weren't even trying to.

There could be a few reasons for that.

Even though it was more of a Midnight Pack trait to analyze and look for patterns, my human mind was intrigued by the possibilities.

They might be already lost to the rut. Our rejected mate would be in heat that was activated by the High Moon. While it would be far more pungent in human form, it would be strong enough to inspire potential mates to join the chase.

Another possible reason was the alphas *wanted* me to follow. While I had only previously been friends with Vern, I'd grown to learn more about the others during the month Katlyn had been gone. I wouldn't call them friends, but at the moment, they were something like allies.

A common goal had united us, which I suspected would be a reoccurring pattern that the Midnight Pack Alpha, Shadow, had already seen coming.

A howl in the distance broke my thoughts as my entire body froze.

It was a human response to react that way, one that annoyed me.

I have no reason to be afraid of wolves. I am *a wolf.*

Except, right now, I was more human than animal.

"You're going to get us killed," I chided my beast, but he still ignored me.

The potential of death didn't frighten him. The best challenges were ones that put everything on the line.

This was my test, one that I had better pass if I wanted to see another High Moon ever again.

Because without our Goddess, I wasn't even sure where I'd go when I died. There would be no moonlit afterlife if She wasn't there to guide me. Something that I wondered if the other alphas had stopped to consider.

We needed to find the Moon Guardian, and we needed to find her before the Hunters killed any more of our kind.

Or before they found her first.

I was painfully aware that they were still out there.

Fuck, they were probably in this forest biding their time to strike. It had been a tense month, one where the packs had driven them off through sheer force of numbers and superior knowledge of the land.

It concerned me that the Hunters hadn't made a move. It was as if they were waiting to see what we'd do.

Or they had something bigger planned.

Quickening my pace, I followed my mate's trail as best I could. My nose twitched, but failed to pick up anything more than the hint of moonlight on the air that beckoned my wolf. His resolve to test me was just as unwavering as mine when it came to the Goddess.

The fact that he hadn't overtaken my body in the shift

proved that we were kindred spirits. In this case, though, it was a detriment.

Cursing him, I kept going. Every second was precious and I couldn't afford to waste time tracking a dead-end trail.

So I moved slowly, making sure I was going the right way by evidence of lithe, barely disturbed wolf prints nearly wiped out by alpha claws that were in pursuit.

I paused when I stepped into a deeper print—one made by a boot.

Humans didn't come this far north, so that meant I was right. The Hunters were out here.

I was trapped in a moment of indecision as the boots took a sharp right, diverting from the wolf tracks.

Were they going to create an ambush?

Even if they weren't, they were clearly in the vicinity and they posed a risk to my mate.

I took one step toward the Hunter path, then hesitated, looking back the way the Moon Guardian had gone.

A longing to follow her all but consumed me, but hadn't I prepared all my life for this sort of ability? One where I overrode the instincts that drove shifters on the High Moon to protect my pack?

Because Katlyn was a member of my pack.

No, not just a member.

My Queen.

Baring my teeth, I overrode my instinct with the decision of what I had to do.

I followed the Hunter tracks with new determination and vowed to do whatever it took to keep them away from Katlyn.

Even if it meant another alpha would Claim her tonight.

Even if it meant I died protecting her.

It was for the Moon Goddess, and I would prove my loyalty to her no matter the cost.

Because even without my wolf to guide me, she was *mine*.

KANE

Run, little moon.

Run like the wind.

And if you're good, I'm going to catch you and make you scream.

I'd made my Moon Guardian a promise, but fuck, She wasn't going to make this easy for me.

Her speed shocked me. I was also impressed by how well She hid Her tracks. It was almost as if She didn't weigh anything at all as She flew through the forest.

But She was an Omega in heat, making Her simple for my nose to follow. Even if I couldn't see the path She might have taken, I could easily let Her intoxicating aroma of jasmine mixed with the silver mist of the High Moon guide me.

Pride from my wolf swelled in my chest, as did his excitement for when we would taste Her again.

But my human mind understood how this was dangerous.

This was Valiance Pack territory. I did not fear Vern or

his pack, but rather what was hidden in this patch of forest. I knew it well enough from the many maps I had studied, as well as my experience running through it before the war.

Which meant I knew about the old Hunter traps that had been placed further up.

I slowed to a stop when I scented water. There was a creek that separated three different territories. The apex led to a sacred pool that had remained untouched since the Hunters had prevented my pack from seeking its power during the war.

How quickly the packs forgot their own history. We had been ostracized because of our intermingling with Hunter blood.

Yet it was the Hunters who had rejected us first, choosing to weaken us by betraying our trust. They were the ones who had walled off this sacred space and it was suicide to try and navigate it now.

Still, my little moon's scent went straight toward that delicious aroma of light-infused waters.

A growl rumbled low in my throat, because She was too fast. Too confident in Her abilities for me to warn Her.

Unless, She was already there.

Little moon... I tested, but She couldn't hear me.

A heaviness had been lingering in my soul, and I wasn't sure if that was my separation from Kaitsja for an entire month, or something more sinister.

Or, perhaps it was simply the fact that She'd entered sacred ground too permeated with magic to hear my call.

But that was a good thing. It meant She had made it to

the creek. A feat that proved She was indeed the Goddess, because none of my wolves had made it to the blessed waters. Not even my own brother.

Is this my test? I asked Her, wondering if I was meant to venture into danger to prove my worth.

Instead of my mate's response, an alpha's growl reverberated through the air. My fur spiked and a responding snarl rumbled in my throat.

The other three had finally caught up to me and seemed to be overturning their decision to respect me as their leader.

Evident by the Valiance Pack Alpha squaring off and showing me his teeth. The moonlight filtered through his sleek gray coat. His green eyes locked onto mine with obvious challenge.

His muscles flexed as if he intended to walk around me, but I stepped in his way.

Me first, I thought at him.

Whether or not Kaitsja intended to keep these alphas, I would establish my position.

They would fall in line or die.

Vern couldn't hear me, but he understood my intent. His muscles coiled as the full power of his wolf sprang into the air, sending the wind crackling with energy.

Normally, I wouldn't indulge in a frontal attack. Still, I would prove my superiority to this wolf and any who challenged me. I had bested all of them once before, followed by Hunters who had come after me.

Of course, I had been blessed by the Goddess at the time. Right now, I only had the power of the High Moon to fuel me.

It put me on more of an even playing field with the Valiance Pack Alpha and my body slammed into his as we collided.

He snarled as I sank my teeth into his shoulder. Pain bloomed across my back when he returned the favor.

Blood flooding my mouth, my wolf came out to play as primal instincts took over. I was already subjected to the rut and the desire to chase my mate, and fighting for Her honor only solidified my resolve.

It would have been an even match, except the other two alphas decided to join in.

I'd fought four of them at once, and now it was just three with Ryker being left behind.

Jaws clamped down on my left leg and another set of teeth dug into my flank.

Fury rose in me as I launched into the air with my adversaries still locked onto my flesh. My body broke and shifted as I sailed upward, because I needed to be in human form.

My chance at winning would be determined by how much moonlight I could absorb, and that worked best through thinner skin unimpeded by fur.

I was Alpha of the Moon Pack, a sect of wolves that lived and breathed Her power, resulting in a magical edge that set us apart from the rest.

It turned our fur white.

It made us powerful, even if it hadn't been enough to help us overcome the numbers of the other four packs; not after we'd been denied access to Moon Creek, among other restrictions placed by the Hunters.

But three alphas? I had enough power to handle that.

Stretching my fingers up through the silver rays, I soaked it in and magic crackled down my spine.

The alphas immediately unlatched and yipped in pain. They weren't designed for Her raw magic like I was.

That's why I would always be first. That's why I would always be *superior*.

Gravity took over, sending us all careening toward the ground. The fight had taken us too far north, which put us at risk of landing in nearby Hunter traps.

I twisted, managing to skid off a tree before landing on the soft soil.

A violent snap of magic and an accompanying howl told me that one of the other alphas hadn't been so lucky.

My bones cracked as I forced my shift to complete a full transition into my human form. The intention was to secure my place, not kill my competition.

Kaitsja had chosen these alphas, spared their lives, and accepted their aid when it came time to rescue Her from the Hunter's cave.

Hell's Heart, they'd called it, but a cave to my senses, nonetheless.

For that, they deserved to live.

"Stay still," I ordered Vern who had fallen into the trap. Its golden runes stretched around him and dug into his fur, sinking invisible teeth into his skin.

An arrow screamed through the air, twisting it open like a split river.

My reflexes were already heightened, thanks to the moonlight I had absorbed, so I easily caught it in my fist.

Then immediately regretted it.

A growl rumbled in my chest when the arrow's wood

burned my skin and sent a rush of fiery magic through my body. I dropped it without hesitation, but the damage was already done.

A Hunter silently stepped through the tree line. His orange eyes glowed with magic and a bow rested loosely in his grip.

He readied another arrow, not taking his gaze off of me.

This was why the wolves had lost against the Hunters before. It was why their betrayal was so dangerous.

They knew far too much about our kind. That was their job. This Hunter knew how my magic worked and all he had to do was disrupt my connection with the moon.

Something the magic in his arrows was spelled to do, apparently.

Inadvertently, the poison from the arrow's touch seemed to affect my connection to Kaitsja as well. I didn't know if that was intentional, but it was even worse than muting my Moon Magic.

I narrowed my eyes and bared my teeth, angry for the disruption to my mate and the dampening of my power.

For the Hunter's sake, it was a disruption that had better not be permanent.

And if he liked his head attached to his body, he would comply with any demand I gave him.

"I'll give you three seconds to give me an antidote to your little parlor trick magic," I warned as Shadow and Dash took up my flank, both still as their wolves.

Just a moment ago, they were ready to take their

pound of flesh, but nothing united the wolves like a Hunter.

The male in question tilted his head as scarred lips stretched in a sideways grin. "Or what?" he asked. He nocked the arrow, then took aim. "Are you going to growl me to death?"

He released the arrow, but not at me.

It split the air again with incredible speed as it sailed toward its intended target.

Vern couldn't move, not while he was still stuck in one of the magicked traps. He roared in pain when the arrow lodged itself into his flank. Magic rippled through his fur, disrupting his ability to remain in wolf form.

But he wasn't dead, at least.

I knew the Hunter had better aim than that. He wasn't trying to kill us.

He was trying to detain us.

Shadow seemed to pick up on that as he edged closer. He stood between the injured alpha and the Hunter as he reared backward, deftly changing into his human physique with a gracefulness that some might envy. "What do you want with us?" he asked, getting straight to the point.

Dash inched forward, but I bumped his muzzle with my palm, then jerked my chin toward Vern.

Dash was a Soldier Alpha. His prowess in battle was useless here, but he might be able to wrench the trap free through brute force.

As much as I wanted to teach Vern a lesson, that was a pointless venture if the Hunters captured us.

Because they'd be going after Kaitsja next, and that was unacceptable.

Another arrow sailed through the air, this one coming from the shadows within the forest.

Shadow blurred with impressive speed, but even with quick reflexes, the arrow still brushed his naked thigh, leaving a crimson streak.

He snarled and favored his good leg as the magic burned through him. Fur sprouted across his arms, but his bones didn't break.

It seemed that he'd been dosed with enough magic to prevent him from shifting again.

Vern roared from behind me just as a snap of metal followed.

Good, the soldier is useful for something, at least.

Not having to protect Vern any longer, I instantly shifted back into wolf form, able to override the poison.

Only because I was an alpha of the Moon Pack. If the others were struck enough times, they'd become useless.

And I realized that was the point.

The Hunter in my sights stiffened when I came at him, all claws and teeth.

He didn't expect me to be able to shift again.

Maybe they don't know everything, after all.

The Hunter tried to release another arrow, but it was too late. I'd surprised him, and that would be his downfall.

My canines sank into his jugular and I *ripped*.

Hunters could come back from a lot, but beheading? Not even a Hunter could survive that.

While I sawed at my victim, a roar of men and Hunters

surrounded us, assuring me I didn't have much time to finish the job.

An arrow raced toward me, but Vern was faster.

He took the arrow in his other shoulder and grunted as it dug into his flesh.

My human mind was surprised. I didn't expect the other alphas to take a Hunter's arrow for me.

But it's not for me, my mind reminded myself. It was for Kaitsja.

They had come to the same conclusion as I had. The Hunters knew we were mated to the Goddess, and they were trying to use us to get to Her.

Whether that meant tapping into our connection with Her, or drawing Her out through our pain, it didn't change the realization of what I had to do next.

Kill.

Kill them all.

It only took three snaps of my mighty jaw to complete my task, and then I dove into the forest as I let my wolf fully take charge.

I rarely let him out to play.

Because my beast was a ferocious, bloodthirsty monster when left unchecked.

And lately, it only seemed to be getting worse. That darkness in the pit of my soul festered with a bloodstone core.

Something that I hid from my pack. Something that I rarely even admitted to myself. I always exuded calmness and confidence.

I never lost my composure.

I never gave in to my temper.

I never let my wolf be in charge.

But now my Goddess was being threatened. Our reason for being. Our *mate*. She would be safe at Moon Creek, but not for long.

I let you free, my wolf.

Rip their spines in half and present their hearts to our Queen.

Tear their flesh and feast on their entrails, because tonight, the High Moon sets.

And the Blood Moon dawns.

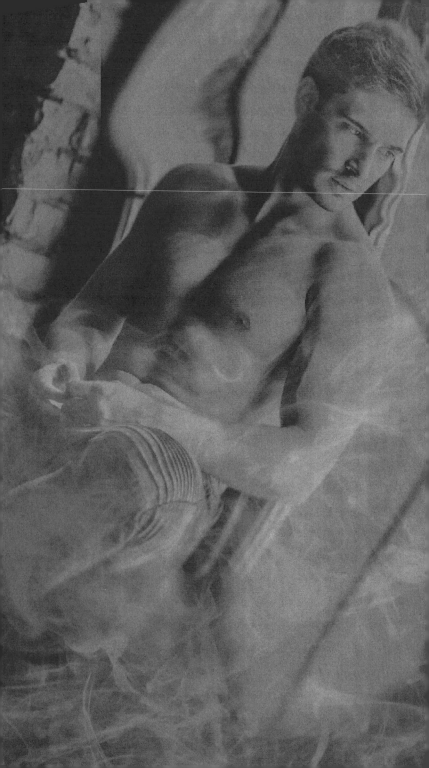

DANTE

I stopped the painstaking work of navigating the moonlit forest when the silver tones above me changed color.

To red.

That can't be good, I thought, glancing up. None of my informants had told me of something like this happening.

We'd been preparing for the High Moon for the past month. It was when the wolves were at their strongest, but in some ways, it was when they were at their weakest, too.

Because not all the wolves were against us. Thanks to my generals, we had worked out a division among the packs. Xenos had been the first of the leaders I'd brought on. However, after our embarrassing defeat, I'd summoned the rest.

Which was how we'd managed to make an unlikely alliance with four of the leaderless wolf packs.

They didn't like the fact that their alphas had been enslaved to a corrupted Goddess.

I had to be careful about that part. All the wolves

revered their deity, but they didn't have to know I meant to kill her. Only that their alphas had failed them. They'd abandoned them and now had joined the Outcast Pack. They would feed on the remains of their lost Goddess for their own power and greed.

It didn't matter if that wasn't true. It was the story I had to sell to save them.

Whether they believed me or not, I wasn't here to kill the wolves. I was here to hunt a monster.

I was here to stop Calamity.

Because a corrupted Goddess was only the start of what Calamity could do. This was not something I would not allow to spread.

Power-hungry alphas had been an easy theory to make. It didn't take long for my informants to learn of the last High Moon Ceremony where a human had infiltrated their ranks and crushed the heart of the Goddess right in front of them all. An impressive feat, to be sure. One I wasn't so convinced she had done on her own.

Regardless, the Moon Goddess had been changed. To the wolves, she was fractured, not dead. The moon still held power, they could still shift—evidenced by their abilities tonight.

They needed hope and a belief that she could be saved.

That was how I had gained their support to let me try to extract the Goddess from the human who had taken her. And how I'd earned allies to guard Moon Creek while I tracked her. Holding her hostage in Hell's Heart hadn't been enough to do the job. So I was trying a different route.

On that front, everything was going according to plan.

But the bloody tones melting down from a starless sky was not a part of any strategy I was aware of.

What are you up to? I wondered, gazing up at the ruby moon.

Was this the Goddess showing her true colors? I had expected something dark, like an eclipse.

This was different.

Not from the Goddess, I decided as I snapped a limb out of my path to walk around a trap. *Not directly.*

The scent of blood made me freeze. It was faint. I was deep within protected territory, so wolves wouldn't be following me here.

But it wasn't wolf blood that lingered on the moonlit air.

It was Hunter blood.

A metallic ring sent a single note through the forest as I withdrew my dagger. The packs were supposed to guard this area, but it was entirely possible that there had been a complication.

Perhaps they'd changed their minds.

Or maybe they simply weren't cut out to stand up against the Corrupted alphas.

Either way, I stayed alert as I pulled the compass from my waistband.

The flame arrow spun a few times before lingering northeast, then seemed to lose its way again.

Her mates were in the woods and they had absorbed moonlight. My estimate was they were the ones interfering with the signal, but I still opted to continue northeast, in the direction the arrow had struggled.

It was off my intended path, forcing me to double back

a few times. I angled around a series of traps as my boot crunched over dried roots on this untouched side of the forest.

Another twig snapped, but it wasn't because of me.

I hadn't been trying to hide my footsteps. No one should have been out here, but that assumption had been wrong.

Pausing, I stilled every muscle in my body to become one with the shadows. My heart slowed to hide my presence as I flexed my fingers around the hilt of my blade.

A human would be doused with adrenaline right now, but I wasn't human.

I was a Hunter, and whoever was here was a fool to face me.

Slipping into the darkened parts of the forest, I tracked the newcomer.

The wind was shifting east, and even though I didn't have a shifter's nose, I would have still picked up the scent of someone within my vicinity.

Meaning my new "companion" was east, as well.

My fingers tingled with anticipation as I kept to the shadows and headed toward the dead man, or woman.

Because whoever it was would be dead very soon.

I paused to examine my surroundings, finding myself barricaded by moonlight on three sides.

Can't proceed this way, I thought, but then I noticed a strange black feather on the ground.

It glimmered with familiar magic that I would recognize anywhere.

My heart stuttered with fear, because this feather belonged to Lily, my mate.

"Hello, Dante," a voice said, making me whirl in a practiced move to slice my attacker.

Only I stopped when I realized it was Logan.

The blade lingered at his throat as a thin line of blood trickled down his bare collarbone and over his muscular chest.

"I could have killed you," I growled.

Logan didn't seem very concerned. "And I could have killed you while you stumbled through the forest like an elephant. You're getting lax in your old age, Hunter," he said with a wry smile I wanted to slap off his face.

Instead of pulling the knife away, I kept it right where it was.

Because Logan was up to one of his games, and I didn't have time to play.

"I assume you're here to stop me?" I asked, already knowing the answer.

I just needed to keep him talking while I figured out how to incapacitate him so I could get the job done.

Logan had grown more powerful after bonding with Lily, just as I had.

She brought out the best in all of us.

Sometimes the worst, too, which Logan demonstrated as he bared his sharp teeth. "Your powers of intuition astound me, Dante."

Logan was in one of his moods. I could tell.

"Is the High Moon fucking with you, Logan?" I asked him as I leaned in.

Electricity charged between us. We were two males in the same mate-circle. While I often spent more quality time with Hendrik than any of the others, Logan had a primal appeal tonight that could prove distracting.

I didn't have time for distractions.

He threw his head back and howled as his response, the sound rippling through my chest and forcing me to my knees.

Not the effect I expected, but we were in his territory now, and it seemed he was enjoying it.

"I'd say so," he said as he knelt on one knee. He slipped his clawed fingers through my hair and lightly scratched my scalp. "This feeling… it's intoxicating, Dante. If I had known this is what it would be like—"

"You never would have known Lily," I finished for him as I forced my muscles to obey. I looked up into his face, taking in the gold ring around his irises that overtook Lily's fiery power.

Surely she'd feel the disruption and come to put an end to this madness, but by then it might be too late.

The Goddess had to die tonight and I was the one to do it.

With all that was going on, and the distraction I had set up for our mate, it would take some time for her to make her way to this realm.

Meaning I was on my own.

"Or you," Logan said, running his claw under my chin to stare into my defiant face. "Or perhaps we would have met, just under different circumstances. Ones where I would be more inclined to kill you rather than fuck you."

"Is that what you want to do to me now?" I asked him, feeling the bond between us tighten and create a stranglehold on my cock. "Kill me? Or fuck me?"

He grinned and leaned in close enough for his hot breath to caress my lips. "Kaito always says there's a fine line between love and hate. That line is the tip of your blade tonight, Hunter." He replaced his breath with the trace of his tongue over my lower lip. "Tell me, what were you doing to the Moon Guardian for the past month? And why do you pursue her now?"

My body refused to move, completely held captive by Logan's seduction.

I wasn't sure if it was our link through the mate-circle, or the power he held because of the High Moon, but I *felt* its energy. He was truly in his element here and he had already been a force to contend with in Hell.

Now, he might just be unstoppable, and that danger appealed to my tastes more than the wolf ever had before.

"I've been trying to do the right thing. She holds a Corrupted deity within her, Logan," I said, hoping to reach him with the truth. "She cannot be allowed to live."

A low rumble vibrated in Logan's chest. "You know I cannot allow you to kill the Goddess that created me, right?"

My legs ached as I attempted to stand, but Logan's howl still resonated within my body. The magic he'd just released forced me to bend to his will because he was an alpha here. Well, he'd always been an alpha, but he'd never been quite this formidable.

"You don't have a choice," I told him as I rewired my magic to counter his power.

He might be strong here, in the realm of his birthright, but he wasn't familiar with its overpowering energy.

I, on the other hand, had spent the last month with the

51

Moon Goddess herself. Her power was unique and something I had to understand in order to accomplish my goal.

Various tests had proven to me that the Moon Goddess had finite strength. The Corruption had empowered her, but also spread her out like oil on the top of the ocean. There were gaps and breaks into the softer, more delicate parts of her power, if one knew where to look.

By letting fate run its course, she had sought out Moon Creek like I knew she would. She needed to restore her magic.

She needed to feast.

And after gluttony came the crash. She might be strong now, but if she was pushed back into human form too soon, it would lull her Goddess into a state of satiated silence.

There would be nothing she could do to stop my blade.

To stop what *needed* to happen.

It would leave the human to fend for herself, and that was my plan. That was why I had to strike tonight.

Everything I had learned in the past month had guided my hand.

It had also taught me how Moon Magic worked. It had a rise and a fall, as well as primal energy that could be manipulated and guided.

Logan had a weakness, and this was the first time in our shared existence I was going to exploit it.

"You're the one without a choice," Logan promised as he scratched his claws down my throat. He palmed the scar across my neck, the one that our mate had put there.

Violence was the bedrock of our relationships and tonight would be no different.

"We'll see who is right, then," I said as I leaned into his touch, allowing his claws to draw blood.

I angled my blade and I carved a rune into the ground; one that called upon the storms that plagued this region.

They moved with massive cracks in the sky, lighting up the forest with flashes of angry blasts.

But that was the only illumination, because the moon was blocked out, causing Logan to lose his hold.

And that's when I struck.

Sorry, wolf.

The Goddess is mine.

KATLYN

A few minutes earlier...

Don't run, the Goddess said inside my head.

My wolf didn't entirely agree, leaving me as the tie-breaker to decide what we were going to do.

I'd let the Goddess lead us this far, so I decided to listen. Only my fur moved with the breeze as I remained rigid, my eyes on the encampment below my vantage point.

The wolf's spirit inside of me desperately wanted to flee.

Alphas, she insisted as if I couldn't smell them. There were hundreds, and once the wind shifted, they would scent *me*.

But it didn't make sense.

How are there more alphas? I asked. *I thought only the leaders of the wolf packs claimed that role?*

The Goddess hummed inside my head. *Usually, yes. But*

I did not design wolves to live without leadership. The packs have been without their alphas for a full moon.

While I contemplated the Goddess's words, my wolf forced my muscles to move. She didn't run back in the direction we had come, but rather led us closer to the cliff's edge as we sniffed the air. So much information flooded my senses as I took in all of the different tastes and smells.

Blood.

Metal.

Sweat.

Fear.

Instinct demanded that I run. My wolf was in heat, meaning we couldn't maintain this state of inaction for very long. My literal temperature was rising by the second, making me feel as if I was on fire.

Alphas are emerging, I guessed.

My wolf growled in agreement.

Yes, the Goddess confirmed. *And if they manage to claim you tonight, it won't matter if your alphas are still alive. It will signify a fight to the death must take place. And these alphas won't be so willing to share.*

Meaning that Kane was in danger, too.

As if thinking of him activated our connection, my heart twisted and I momentarily *felt* him.

There was something horribly wrong, because this wasn't the Kane I knew.

A bloodthirsty hunger threatened to devour me, running through me like the lightning from the storms as my breath hitched.

I shut off the connection before I fell prey to it. When I glanced up, I realized I hadn't imagined it.

The moon was red.

Conflicting emotions battled inside of my rapidly beating heart. Whatever was going on with Kane, I hoped he would figure it out.

Because I feared if he found me in such a state, he might do more harm than good.

My nostrils twitched as I picked up a fresh wave of more alphas on their way, circling my location as they looked for a way in.

What if I stay in wolf form? I asked. *Then I can't be claimed, right?*

My wolf seemed to pace in the back of my mind.

You won't be able to stop the change. It's a High Moon and you have feasted on my power. Your wolf won't stay lucid for much longer as the heat overtakes her... overtakes both *of you.* She drew in a deep breath. *And if an alpha finds you in such a state...*

I'll be forced to shift, I finished.

That's how I designed the wolves, she confirmed. *It creates the strongest mate pairings. It ensures the continuity of a race that I had created, a race I had blessed. My blessings have been abused and perverted. Something we will remedy once the packs are united, as they should be.*

Right, assuming I survived the night.

This is bullshit, I told her.

She remained silent, which I took for agreement.

I hadn't survived a month in Hell just to come back and be taken by the first wolf that found me.

What about the traps? I asked. *If they can't get past them, we should be safe, right?*

The Goddess didn't get a chance to answer me. A clap of thunder rolled over the cliff face and rippled the waters. Another bolt hit, this one leveling a patch of forest to the south.

The wind shifted as a storm seemed to come out of nowhere, dark clouds whirling into existence with angry sparks of lightning ripping through the darkness. A sense of dread washed over me as the billowing plumes blocked out the moon.

My power immediately waned the moment I lost my connection to the celestial object. It was the source of my power and my biggest strength.

Without it, I was left to maintain off of finite reserves. Yes, I had feasted on magic, but the majority of that had healed internal injuries and renewed my energy that had been dangerously depleted.

Meaning, most of that power was already gone.

Damn it all.

The storms were always a thorn in my side and it seemed tonight would be no different.

The Goddess sounded groggy inside my head without the power of moonlight to awaken her.

Kaitsja, she pressed, her tone growing frantic as she faded from my mind. *Something's wrong. Something dark is—*

A pop sounded from behind me, making me flinch in its direction.

The dark clouds stretched high into the night. Fear gripped my chest as clusters of brilliant hunter traps began to detonate in sequence. It was as if they were running a course around the mountain, exploding like firecrackers in a domino effect of destruction.

The traps, she hissed. *Without them, the alphas will come for you. They'll come for us.*

Then we fight, I thought back at her. *If I die, then at least I'll take some damned wolves with me.*

I was learning not to hate the wolves, especially now that I was one of them, but damn it all if they were going to ruin everything.

You don't understand, she pressed as her voice grew weaker. *If something happens to you, I will no longer be contained. Calamity will take me and the storms you see now will be a mild breeze compared to the torrent to come.*

With that ominous warning, the wind picked up, sending smoke and debris over the treetops. My wolf growled louder, her fur bristling as she prepared to face the multitude of enemies that now had access to us.

Unwanted alphas vying for power.

Hunters who wanted me dead.

And humans that would not understand what I had become or the force they would unleash if I was killed.

I couldn't let that happen. My family was still out there.

Kane was still out there.

There were still people I loved worth protecting.

I allowed my wolf to take charge. She knew this body better than I did, but we both felt clumsy in it without the guidance of the Goddess within us.

Leaving the dull creek behind, I cautiously made my

way down the mountain. It wasn't anything like when I'd bounded my way up here.

The Goddess had been guiding my footsteps and without her, I felt like a child lost in a dark, unfamiliar place.

Not unlike when I'd been lost in the woods, once, long ago.

My older sister whose memory was buried deep in a tiny box I never opened seemed to guide me now that the Goddess was asleep.

If you're lost, I'll find you.

Her promise wrapped around me with a warmth that I knew I imagined. My body burned with the effects of my wolf's condition while an icy wind threatened to rip any heat from my fur.

Back then, I hadn't understood how close I had come to being lost forever. But now, as fear clawed at my throat and my chance for escape dwindled around each bend, I felt a similar sense of dread.

My wolf slowed her pace as we neared the bottom of the mountain. The wind had shifted and I could no longer smell the alphas, but I could smell others.

Hunters. Humans.

But not my mates.

Where are they?

The wind whistled through the trees and a new fog hung low on the ground like a blanket—obscuring my view of anything beyond it.

I didn't have to see to know I wouldn't be alone much longer.

A howl ripped through the silence, sending shivers

down my spine. My heart raced as I paused, waiting to see which direction I needed to run.

But the Goddess had warned me *not* to run, right?

Was I going to have to fight?

An enormous beast with shining white fur emerged from the darkness, making me sigh in relief.

Althea.

Only she wasn't alone. Her chest heaved and air puffed against the cold in front of her muzzle, betraying her rapid breaths. When she spotted me, she nodded once, then she twisted to face the fog.

She snarled in warning just as wolves broke through next, one slamming into her and pinning her to the ground. She didn't stay pinned long, though. She was the seer of the Moon Pack and a blast of light surged into the sky, burning the wolf that had pinned her alive.

There were many more to take his place.

The alphas had found me, and they were determined not to leave empty-handed.

Althea couldn't hold them all off. Moonlight flashed again, only keeping a portion of them at bay. The rest came at me like a wall of teeth and claws. I dropped and snapped my maw, locking onto flesh and tasting blood, but I was quickly yanked away.

I was a tiny Omega in a circle of alphas and all of them wanted me.

I'm not a prize to be claimed, I thought, angry at the turn of events.

Tonight was supposed to be a redemption for my mates. Not a contest for any wolf with balls to enter.

My heart was not for sale to the highest bidder.

Although, it was apparent these wolves weren't interested in my heart. Their growls reverberated through my body, enticing me to run.

And if I ran, they would chase.

It would start a series of events that would end with me claimed by a bite and an alpha's knot. They would take my power, and with it they would abuse my gifts.

They would kill anyone who stood in their way.

Althea was still alive. Her moonlight blasts continued to light up the sky, but I knew she couldn't keep this up. Perhaps they weren't intending to kill her, but to keep her as a runner-up prize. From my understanding, she wasn't mated, either.

The alphas encircled me, each one desperate for dominance to lay claim for their pack.

Althea howled again in warning—or maybe it was a signal.

If she had reinforcements on the way, they had better hurry.

I bared my teeth, warning the alphas to back off. Of course, that only seemed to spur them on.

They were too focused on me, too blinded by their own desires.

I howled again as lightning from the clouds snapped through the air. The moon was behind it and damned if these storms would keep me from my source of power.

A glimmer of a single ray of bloody moonlight broke through the sky, only briefly.

But it was enough. And for the moment, I was grateful for whatever Kane had done to it, because it was *powerful*.

The alphas lunged. Raw energy rippled through my

limbs as the spirit within me whispered guidance, giving me speed and agility to evade.

I was small, but quick.

And I was a fucking Goddess.

I conjured up a shield of energy and a shimmering wall of silver moonlight sizzled around me. The alphas snapped at it. Their massive maws popped the air as they tried to gnaw their way through, but it held.

My victory was short-lived as an arrow careened through the shield that had been designed for wolves, not men.

"Hold!" a voice chided, but another arrow came, singing by my ear and leaving a slice of pain as it grazed the delicate skin at my temple.

The members of my village had come, and they wanted me dead.

And could I blame them? I had become the embodiment of the power that made the wolves so dangerous.

But the storms won't stop with my death, I remembered.

The storms would only get worse. The Goddess was contained within me and if I died, she would be set free once again.

And then she would be at the mercy of the force that had come for her, the one the Hunters called Calamity.

My heart pinched when I recognized some of the men and women from my village.

Harlan.

Jared.

Persilla.

Don't look at their faces, my wolf instructed. *Look at their weapons.*

She was right. Each of them held an object.

Harlan had an axe that he often used to chop wood for my family.

Jared held a dagger he used to skin the rabbits I brought him.

And Persilla held a bow, the very same one she had used to teach me archery.

I watched her fingers as she nocked another arrow and aimed it my way.

Every muscle in my body froze as time seemed to slow down. Hunters broke through the fog next, taking up the backlines behind the villagers.

Which meant if I could reach them, I could cause enough of a distraction to escape.

I knew Harlan, Jared, Persilla, and all the other faces that were making a wide circle around me. The alphas ignored them, but I didn't see this ending in their favor.

Humans always earned the short end of the stick.

Persilla aimed, but she didn't seem to be able to get a good lock on me. Althea was sending rays of moonlight to blur the area.

What do I do? I asked. I wasn't sure if I was asking the Goddess, my wolf, or myself.

The Goddess was still silent, leaving me to rely on my instincts and the memories of my sister's teachings.

Right now, that meant listening to my heart. And my heart was telling me to give the humans a chance.

My bones snapped and everyone seemed to hear it. Wolves perked their ears and leaned my way. Humans paused, and the Hunters behind them drew their blades.

My vision changed as everything grew darker, but

sharper. My sense of smell practically vanished and left me only capable of noticing the moist moss from the creek that competed with the musk of the forest.

I reared back my head and howled, the sound quickly changing to a scream.

And then a hand clamped over my mouth—a human one—as I was dragged away.

And all hell broke loose.

The male behind me easily dragged me away from the fight and deeper into the forest.

I tried to fight, but I was too disoriented now in my human form.

And my heat was hitting with a vengeance.

Pain unlike anything I'd ever felt before twisted my stomach, sending invisible knives ripping through my core.

When the hand lifted from my mouth, I turned in the male's grip, expecting to see an alpha.

And in my current state, that both relieved and horrified me.

But I went still when I recognized the specter that couldn't exist.

Brown hair draped over familiar brown eyes that were speckled with green, always reminding me of the forest we had come from.

My breath caught as I forced out the name.

"…Charlie?"

SHADOW

Four hours later...

"Katlyn better be alive or I'm going to kill all of you out of spite," I grumbled.

Although, Kane would probably get to us first.

"You can try," Dash said as his bare feet shuffled through the forest, but there wasn't any humor in his tone.

We were all tired, pissed off, and trying to get through the shit show that was last night's High Moon that once again left us without our mate.

But not without killing. We'd done plenty of that.

As far as High Moon's went, it was not what I would call a successful night. If it even counted as a High Moon after what we'd witnessed, anyway.

I looked up as the last of the red rays disappeared. I'd never seen a Blood Moon before, but it didn't mean I'd never heard of one.

When the Blood Moon set, red still remained. Bodies lay strewn across the now crimson forest floor. Hundreds of bodies.

Wolves. Hunters. Humans.

Death has no discrimination. I'd always known that. Death's lesson was one I was intimate with. After the loss of my father, my mother had disappeared.

I knew now it was because I was not yet of age, so she feared being taken by an even worse brute than my father had been. We'd already become familiar with the massacre of a neighboring family. They were ones we'd known since we'd been mere pups.

The fallout was simple enough. An alpha was not pleased when his mate died during childbirth, so he killed any females from her line as a result.

I'd lost a friend that night and that was when I'd started learning how to suppress my emotions.

Because his words still haunted me.

Our pack needs successful breeders, not empty wombs.

It was disgusting. My father had done nothing to stop it, and if my mother had experienced the same difficulties, I had no doubt we would have met the same fate.

But her instinct to flee had left me alone, so I'd searched for her. She had trusted me to survive, but I did not give her that same level of faith on her own.

It was how I had met the strange wolf from another realm. Logan was unlike any alpha I had ever met and when I had been searching for death, he was who I had found.

Logan had saved my life—and hers. His protection

until I was old enough to take care of my family was a debt that could never be paid.

In exchange, I had taught him the ways of the Midnight Pack and our Goddess. An alpha like Ryker likely would have been a better choice for the latter task. The Mystic Alpha trailed behind me, his bare feet leaving a bloody path to add to the carnage.

"Keep up," I told him.

He growled in response, but it didn't have any force behind it.

Because his wolf had abandoned him.

Mine had forgiven me once we'd found Katlyn, but not Ryker's. Ryker's spirit was loyal to the Goddess to a fault, even to his own detriment. He was going to have to figure his shit out.

"Leave Ryker be," Vern said. "He's the only one of us to remain in human form tonight—and he still saved our asses. You owe him your thanks."

I huffed a noncommittal reply, because I knew Vern was right.

After Kane had ripped through the initial wave of Hunters, we'd fallen right into an ambush only for Ryker to take out the archer that would have sent an arrow straight through my brain.

And he'd done it as a worthless human with a stolen knife.

I didn't like being saved. Logan was different. I'd been a pup. Now I was supposed to be an alpha and the leader of my pack.

And now that the Blood Moon had set, the storms

subsided, and a foggy sun had started to rise, we continued through the trail of bodies searching for Kane.

And hoped that Katlyn was with him.

Vern, Ryker, Dash, and I trudged along in silence.

The sounds of birds chirping, the scent of lingering Moon Blossoms, and the crisp morning breeze couldn't extinguish the reality of blood soaking the ground.

It was hard to believe that *one* wolf had done this.

I'd seen Kane's true power when he'd fended off all of us in combination with the army of Hunters, but he hadn't lost control like this.

He was the only one of us mated to Katlyn—the Goddess herself—and there was no telling what that had done to him.

Was this a side-effect of mating a Goddess?

Or was this Kane's true nature?

That question soured in my stomach as the trail of death eventually led us to a clearing.

A single figure stood silhouetted against the rising sun that battled through the fog.

It was Kane.

He leaned against a tree as he opened and closed his fists. His chest heaved, rippling muscles caked in blood.

He looked like a god of carnage.

We all paused at a safe distance and waited for him to notice us, but his gaze seemed fixed somewhere in the distance.

His once-white hair was now stained red and hung around his face.

He had the look of an alpha who'd lost himself.

I was the first to approach him. "Kane," I said, testing if he could even hear us.

His wild gaze locked onto me. It took effort not to flinch or turn away. He would respond aggressively in this state to any show of weakness.

"Where's Katlyn?" Ryker demanded from behind me.

Despite not having his wolf, he was still an alpha. He stepped forward, completely fearless, as he challenged the crazed Blood King.

Because that's what he was to me now. A ring of red surrounded his irises where gold should have been and a crown of carnage sent blood trailing over his brow.

The name of our mate seemed to get through to him as he straightened.

"I… lost her," he finally said. His voice came out gravely and inhuman, but the lucid part of him was still in there.

Although deeply, because a tremor ran through his body as he snarled. Fur sprouted on his arms, only to turn back into skin a moment later.

It was as if he was struggling to maintain control over his wolf.

"Can you feel her?" Vern asked, his tone softer than mine would have been. The Valiance Pack had political leanings, and often knew how to handle situations with care when necessary.

Kane was clearly unstable, so unless we wanted our blood added to the forest floor, it was probably wise to let Vern take the lead.

The Moon Pack Alpha sniffed the air. "I can… feel her. Yes. She's alive, but I can't *reach* her."

"I saw humans with the Hunters," Dash offered.

I glanced at him, but Vern voiced the obvious conclusion first. "She returned with them."

"Or they took her," Ryker suggested.

Kane's nostrils flared, not seeming to like either possibility. "Then I will track her down and rip anyone who keeps her from me to pieces."

That probably wasn't the best plan if we wanted Katlyn's favor. The humans were her family. It was a very real possibility that she had willingly gone with them, especially after we had failed to protect her.

"Perhaps we should all go," I offered.

"No," Vern said, making us face him. "If Kane can feel her, that means she's alive. If he can't reach her, that means she doesn't want to talk to us. We have to respect that, and in the meantime…" he glanced meaningfully at the carnage. "Our packs are in disarray. It was a mistake leaving them leaderless."

Ryker crossed his arms and glowered at Kane. "That was likely the Outcast's intention. You wanted all the packs in one place so you could kill them, hmm?" He stalked closer to Kane, disregarding any sense of self-preservation.

Ryker was a formidable wolf, but Kane towered over all of us.

He straightened and glowered down at the Mystic Alpha. "You think I wanted this? I was supposed to lead Kaitsja to glory. She was supposed to unite the packs and bring the best out of me, in *all* of us. I waited for her. I didn't mean for this to happen." He spread his arms and blood dripped from his fingertips. "I never asked for any of it!" he roared, blasting his anger straight into Ryker's face.

Ryker didn't move. Instead he defiantly stared the alpha down.

"Then we fix it, Kane." He clapped one hand on the male's muscular shoulder, painting his own palm red in the process. "Together."

Kane's nostrils flared and his teeth seemed to sharpen. He shouldn't be able to shift after the full extent of a High Moon, but after last night, I wouldn't put anything past him.

His wild gaze slowly drifted to each of us, finally settling on me. "You are the only one who shares my suffering, Shadow. What say you?"

I raised a brow, but it was an astute observation.

I, too, held a beast inside of me that could cause this sort of carnage.

I never let him out.

If I did, I feared I would lose myself completely. Kane had shown strength to keep a semblance of sanity after a night like tonight.

And as much as I hated to admit it, Vern was right. Our packs were fractured and lost, and that was something that needed to be remedied.

I met the gaze of each alpha before responding to Kane. "I say that our packs need us. We are supposed to be their leaders. Their protectors. If we are to be worthy of the Goddess, then we need to fix this."

That was easier said than done. What I wanted to do was exactly what Kane had said. Find our mate and rip into anyone who stood between us.

Even if I wasn't mated to Katlyn, I could sense her heat and her call.

She was in pain. But I had to be stronger than my basic instincts. If I mated her without a pack left to lead, much less without her consent, I was no better than my father who took what he wanted and left nothing but pain and death behind.

I promised myself if I ever became alpha, I'd be nothing like that asshole.

"Then go back to your packs," Kane said, his words obscured by the growl of his wolf. He was overriding his primal instincts, just like the rest of us.

But that's what made us more than simple beasts with a drive for sex and hunger.

The human spirits within us tempered our wolves when required. It was a balance that the Goddess had planned for us to make sure we were the supreme race in this realm.

A balance that we needed to restore.

"We reconvene tonight at Moon Pack headquarters," Kane continued. "I will be sure to instruct any survivors of a truce between the packs."

"And the Hunters?" I ventured. I assumed that the villagers we had encountered were either dead or returned home. The Hunters, though, would still be a problem.

Kane showed his teeth. "Leave them to me."

KATLYN

I woke inside a tangle of blankets and rabbit furs. Nightmares must had plagued me during the night, because the tiny fibers stuck to my sweat-slick body.

Groaning, I rolled onto my side and peeled away a damp layer, exposing my skin to the morning sunlight.

I'd slept in the forest a handful of times. It wasn't the safest place to be, but Charlie always guarded me on those nights I'd been hunting for days at a time and we had been too far from home to make it back before sunrise.

Charlie...

I blinked a few times when I spotted his silhouette against the rising sun. He sat on a rock with his back to me and a blade and sharpening stone in his hands.

Slice.

Slice.

He worked his blade into a fine edge as he maintained his position.

"This is an odd dream," I murmured as I tucked my hands under my face.

Charlie was dead, but dreaming about him didn't seem too unusual, I supposed.

The pain, though, that was odd. Knives twisted in my stomach without warning, making me hiss.

Had I eaten something poisonous?

What had I had for dinner? Was it fish? No, that couldn't be right.

Charlie turned his face, but kept his gaze averted. "Good, you're awake."

I blinked again as I tried to clear my vision.

"Awake?" I repeated.

Because I was definitely still sleeping.

His lips quirked in a sideways grin, giving him attractive dimples that most girls went crazy for.

Charlie and I had always been platonic, but right now I couldn't remember why.

Because when did he get so hot?

"There are some clothes over there," he said, indicating a neatly folded pile of fabric by a burned-out fire pit. He turned, showing me his back again as he returned to his task of sharpening his blade. "Althea gave them to me. Once you're dressed, we can talk."

I stared at him.

Then pinched myself.

"Ouch," I hissed, because I very much felt that.

He glanced over his shoulder again. "Are you hurt?"

Throwing off my blankets, I marched up to him and stopped just behind him.

This can't be real.

He turned a little more, and then his cheeks flushed when he took in my nude state.

I didn't give two shits that I was naked because this was definitely a dream.

And if it wasn't…

Tentatively, I reached out to touch him as I knelt on one knee.

My heart skipped a beat when my fingers met warm, hard man. His heat bled through his fighting leathers. They'd been repaired, but I could still see the claw marks on them.

And there was a light scar across his throat.

Where he'd been mauled.

Where he'd been *killed*.

My vision went blurry as emotion swelled up in my chest. "I think I'm the one who should be asking you that, Charlie."

He turned enough for me to wrap my arms around him and bury my face in his chest. The sobs came without warning.

Because this wasn't a dream.

Charlie's alive!

He shushed me as he held me, easily pulling me into his lap. "It's okay, Kaitsja. I'm here."

Something inside of me stirred when he used my wolf's name.

I'd always hated it. Only my Aunt Daliah had called me that, and Charlie when he wanted to tease me, but now it held a whole new meaning.

It was as if they had both known my destiny.

Sniffling, I pulled away and looked up into his gorgeous brown eyes. The flecks of green reminded me of the forest, as did his scent which seemed even more powerful and alluring now.

Why have I never kissed you? I wondered.

"How are you alive?" I asked, still unable to believe it. "I thought you were dead, Charlie."

He chuckled as he nuzzled his nose against mine. It felt so easy being with him.

So… intimate.

It had never been like this before.

But maybe it could have, had I been willing to explore that option with him.

We're family. We can't damage what we have. Our friendship is everything.

It was a primal fear of mine to lose Charlie over a lover's spat. We'd mockingly been handfasted as children, but now that vow felt more real… more prominent and less of a joke.

"I did die," Charlie said, his breath warm on my lips as he spoke. "But you brought me back."

I frantically tried to remember that night.

Alphas.

My alphas.

Fuck, Kane!

My memories flooded in as my brain attempted a restart, assuring me that this wasn't a dream at all.

I was definitely awake. Charlie was alive, but were my alphas?

I pulled away from his alluring lips. The attraction to him confused me, but then I remembered my wolf had been in heat—no, she *still* was in heat.

My stomach twisted again and I hissed as I curled my fingers into his leathers. "It hurts, Charlie."

"I know," he told me. "Althea warned me your heat might linger." His jaw flexed. "Listen, Kaitsja—"

I curled away from him before he could reject me.

The only reason I was feeling these feelings for Charlie was because of my damned heat.

My wolf.

"I'm sorry. Don't worry about it," I told him as I forced my feet to take me to the pile of clothes. I stepped into the undergarments, then into the tight-fitting leathers. "So, Althea found you?"

He said that I'd brought him back, but I had no recollection of doing any such thing.

But he had eaten a Moon Blossom before his death.

It was possible that I had saved him, somehow.

"She finished what you had started," he told me.

My brows pinched together as I faced him.

He had definitely changed since that night. He was more muscular, less boyish.

Part of his allure had to be real and not just fabricated by my heat, because this was certainly an upgrade from the Charlie I remembered.

"You seem different."

He nodded. "I suppose dying will do that to a person." He shrugged and sheathed his knife as he stood. "I feel different too. I remember my life, but it's like I'm looking back on someone else, you know?"

I canted my head. "Do you remember how long you've been alive?" Because Althea must have helped him revive recently.

Fuck, that's a question I never thought I'd ask.

81

How does one come back to life? I know I'm part goddess now, but that's a whole new level of power.

He shrugged again. "I was only dead for a few hours, I think. And Althea said that it's something that can only happen once a High Moon."

I tried to process that.

It made sense, now that I thought about it. I'd been too weak to even keep myself alive on my own that night as if I'd already expended the majority of my power. And then this past High Moon I had revived myself after near-death in the Hunter's Hell.

Maybe I did actually die.

But one thing in particular bugged me. If Althea helped him the same night he had died…

I fidgeted with my leathers, finding them constricting. "That would mean Althea didn't tell me you were alive."

He hummed in response. "Yes. She told me that you had… wolves, to deal with. I've been preparing the villagers for the war while you were doing 'your part.' Her words."

My stomach twisted, but this time it wasn't just the effect of my lingering heat igniting a fire in my belly.

Althea had kept so much from me, and she had gone as far as sending Charlie back to my village to bring humans to fight.

I knew she was a seer and could have predicted these events, but she had acted on her own accord, because Kane surely didn't know about any of this.

I felt him out there, so he was definitely alive. But our connection was muted, somehow.

I had a feeling that was my own doing.

My wolf was angry with him, as was the quiet Goddess resting in my soul. Something about him perverting her High Moon.

I didn't really care.

Charlie. Is. Alive.

I still couldn't wrap my head around any of this. Kane was alive and I wasn't sure if that comforted me or frightened me. Especially now that I had Charlie back.

A part of me worried for the other alphas I *couldn't* feel, but in the light of day, I wasn't so sure they deserved my concern.

A month ago, I had been plotting their brutal deaths. Had they really earned my forgiveness just because they'd freed me from the Hunter's Hell?

It was their fault I was in this predicament to begin with, anyway. They'd lost control of their packs, evident by the fact that so many alphas had emerged, and all of them had come after me.

"Charlie—" I began, but he cut me off.

"Call me Lyle," he said as he took my hand. When I raised a brow in question, he chuckled. "Like I said, I feel like a different person now. I'd prefer a different name."

"Lyle," I said, testing it out.

His dimples reappeared in reward as he smiled. He seemed to like the way I said his new name.

Surely I'm not imagining this attraction.

Clearing my throat, I reclaimed my hand before I did something stupid, like pull him closer to me. Until my heat had passed, I wouldn't act on my impulses and further embarrass myself.

I'd already thrown my naked body at him and sat in his lap.

Actually, he *pulled you into* his *lap,* my unhelpful mind corrected.

A shout in the distance broke my train of thought, making me snap my attention southward. "Where are we?" I asked, suddenly alert.

"At the village's border," he said, pointing out the familiar moss-lined trees. "I took us to the west side where we don't usually go. I wanted to make sure we had a chance to talk before I took you home."

Home.

A shiver ran up my spine at that realization.

I was going to see my family again.

My sister.

A whole new set of emotions rippled through me, leaving a wake of uneasiness behind. "Am I welcome there?" I asked, my voice softer than it had ever been. If I spoke any louder, it might crack on my pain. I glanced at him, this time allowing myself to become absorbed by his forest-speckled eyes. "Don't they know what I am now?" It had been members of my village trying to kill me last night.

He moved to take my hand again, then seemed to think better of it as he let his fist drop to his side. "Let me deal with that. You're going home and that's the end of it."

I frowned at the bite in his tone, but I knew that anger wasn't reserved for me.

This was a conversation he'd had before with the village elders.

"Char—Lyle… if I'm not welcome back, then I'll leave."

Kane would be coming for me and the last thing I wanted was to bring the wolves to my family's door.

Kane would tear it all to the ground. And if he didn't, the other alphas would.

Lyle's jaw clenched, his eyes darkening with anger. "You have every right to go back to your family. They have no reason to turn you away."

"I'm a wolf now," I said bluntly. I held up my hand and easily brought forth my claws. "That's plenty of reason."

After last night, my wolf and I were closer than we ever had been before. She twisted and turned inside of me, needing a resolution to the High Moon that should have ended in courtship.

Instead, we woke to my childhood protector guarding us from the night.

A human that I had brought back from the dead.

"I know what and *who* you are," he said. "You're Kaitsja, the best archer in the village and a protector who has saved hundreds of lives from the storms. That's who you've always been. The rest is irrelevant."

It was hardly irrelevant, but Charlie—*Lyle*—seemed to be in an argumentative mood.

This time, he didn't hesitate as he stepped forward and wrapped his arms around my elbows, forcing me to look up at him.

Had he grown taller, too?

"Althea told me *how* you became a wolf. You went straight into the heart of their city and crushed the spirit of their goddess right in front of them. You did something all humanity should be thankful for." He leaned in closer and grabbed my chin, forcing me to lift my face. "Be proud of what you've done. Don't hide what strength you've taken from the wolves because it is *ours* now."

My breath hitched as his fingers ran down the column of my throat, resting on my collarbone.

Definitely not imagining the attraction.

"Lyle?" I asked, my voice wavering.

"What is it, Kaitsja?" he asked.

I licked my lips, my throat suddenly feeling dry.

"Can you… can you kiss me?"

If he kissed me, I would know he meant what he was saying. I would know that he truly accepted me, wolf and all.

And if he could accept me, perhaps my family could, too.

He didn't move for a long moment, making me wonder if he was going to reject me just like my alphas did on the first High Moon.

But after an eternity, he closed the distance between us until his lips hovered over mine.

"I'll do anything you ask, Kaitsja. Anything."

And then he kissed me, leaving me on a breathless embrace of heaven as his lips pressed against mine.

LYLE

I've loved Katlyn for as long as I could remember.

Those were the memories that were strongest from my prior life, because I was absolutely a different person now.

Death changed me for the better.

I had always been too meek to tell the love of my life how I truly felt. I'd done everything I could to protect her and be what she needed me to be.

She had always called me her brother, and every time she had said that word it crushed a little piece of my soul.

Because she was so much more to me.

And when she asked me to kiss her, I couldn't believe it.

And even if it was her heat talking, in the moment I was too weak to care.

I needed to kiss her like I needed to breathe. For weeks I had to go through my day-to-day knowing that she thought I was dead.

I had to do the bidding of a white wolf that had helped me take my first breath in my new life.

Oh, it had been painful. But my death had all been part of Althea's plan.

My death drove Katlyn to go after the wolves heart and fulfill her destiny. That was a part of the story that I omitted, for now.

Not Katlyn... Kaitsja, I reminded myself.

I didn't divulge everything that Althea had shared with me, because the white wolf had warned me that Kaitsja needed to learn the truth in pieces. Which was something I was starting to agree with.

My rebirth was already a lot for her to handle.

We walked hand-in-hand back to the village. I'd tucked away her bow behind one of the trees and it felt right with her having it slung over her shoulder.

In some ways, it was as if nothing had changed, except now we were reunited stronger than ever before.

I wanted her.

I wanted to *keep* her.

And if Althea had her way in the end, I would have to let her go.

The plan had been to rise up the village for the war, the one against a Corrupted Goddess.

The Hunters had seemed like an answer to prayers to gods long gone and long dead. They wanted to take out the deity that gave the wolves their magic.

But that was a conundrum in itself. Kaitsja was now one with the Wolf Goddess.

And that's where my approach differed from the Hunters' and the strategy I'd helped plan with the village.

The first part of the plan had been convincing them to ally with the Hunters and even some of the wolves—all of them had the same goal.

Take Kaitsja.

Although, that looked different for each of us.

The Hunters wanted her dead.

As did most of the villagers.

But the wolves wanted her for themselves—as did I.

Except I would always let Kaitsja choose her path. The beasts had done my work for me by trying to force her.

It led her straight into my arms.

Maybe it was just the effects of her heat making her so amenable to my desires, but I wouldn't take advantage of that.

That's why I had stopped the kiss. If she really wanted the same things I did, then I would learn the truth of it in time.

But I would continue to prove myself to her. I had died for her, and I would gladly do it again.

Now, I was going to take her home and convince the village that she was an asset more useful on our side than against it.

Because Althea told me something that the Hunters didn't know—or maybe they just didn't agree with.

If she died, the storms that plagued our lands would only get worse.

My reasons to guard her might be selfish, but that would be a good enough reason as any for the others to want her protected.

If I could convince them, of course. I'd tried without

avail for weeks. They'd marched onward with the intent to kill—not capture.

Now, I had to show them that I was right. Katlyn was still in there and she was an asset to us alive, not an enemy we needed dead.

"Stay close to me," I told her as we reached the warning system around the village. The faint strings could be seen attached to trees and glimmering like thin spiderwebs around the perimeter.

Her aunt had established it and maintained it—even if she did live outside of the main village confines.

Few knew that she did so through magic.

I'd learned the truth upon my return.

Many truths that even Kaitsja didn't know. But she would by night's end.

"I can take care of myself, you know," Kaitsja said as she released my hand so she could free her bow. "I know how to aim to immobilize without killing anyone."

She sure did. She'd demonstrated that on a few villagers who had attempted to steal Moon Blossoms and run.

Not everyone was in full control of their fear. Those who had betrayed our trust were watched and maintained by the village elders and the protectors.

I had been a protector, before. Now, I wasn't sure what I was. I'd become a battle strategist and leader, of sorts. What had once been too difficult for a meek boy was now easy for the reborn man.

Things had changed.

Buildings lined with wilting Moon Blossoms came into view, as did a few familiar faces.

Harlan, a short man with a mean scowl and a penchant for pushing his luck was the first to approach.

He brandished his axe while Kaitsja readied her bow. "What's the meaning of this?" he asked.

"I've brought Katlyn home," I informed him, making sure to use her given name and not the one Daliah preferred.

Jared, a burly man with menacing eyes joined us as more villagers exited their homes. He snarled and spit in my direction. "Boy, you yourself said the goal was to end this war before it began. Why isn't her head severed from her body?"

Rage rippled through me, but Kaitsja answered before I could.

"I'm right here, asshole," she said, drawing an arrow from her quiver. "How many rabbits have I brought your family, Jared? This is the thanks I get?"

His knuckles went white around his short dagger. One he knew how to use when he wanted. I witnessed him in action last night and I wasn't letting him anywhere near Kaitsja with that blade.

"You might sound like Katlyn, but you're not her anymore, are you?" He glowered at her, then narrowed his eyes on me. "Perhaps you're not the same either, Charlie." He held up a hand. "Oh, sorry, it's *Lyle* now, right?"

"Enough," a feminine voice said.

The crowd that had formed parted when Kaitsja's mother came through.

The woman had a presence that demanded respect. Her dark hair was otherwise streaked with silver and her face was weathered from years of hard living on the edge of wolf-owned territory.

But her eyes still held the same sparkle as her daughter's, one that held hope for the future and a day where everything would change.

She believed more than any of us that those days had finally come upon us.

"Mom," Kaitsja said, letting her bow fall to her side as she ran to her and threw an arm around her neck.

"My daughter," she said, burying her face in Kaitsja's hair and inhaling. She ran her fingers through the loose strands, holding her at arms' length. "You're home."

"You should leave her to us," another female said.

Persilla was a thorn in my side. She was the one who always fought me the hardest when I vied to keep Kaitsja alive.

She accented her words now with her bow and aimed the arrow straight for Kaitsja's heart.

Growling, I ripped the bow down, forcing the arrow to face the ground. "Stop it, Persilla. You can see she's no threat. She's fucking hugging her mother, for gods' sake."

Persilla wrinkled her nose. "That *thing* isn't Katlyn." She turned to the pair. "Come on, Naomi. I know you already lost one daughter and losing another is too much to bear, but clinging to that monster isn't going to change reality. Stop being a grief-stricken weakling and face reality, for the safety of what's left of our village."

Naomi clenched onto her daughter. "Do I look grief-stricken to you? I have my wits about me, Persilla. And anyone can see that my daughter has come home a hero, not a *monster*."

The villagers around us rose in a din of arguments, ones that I'd heard a million times before.

I had my allies and my adversaries, but the only opinions that truly mattered weren't here.

"This is a matter for the elders," I reminded everyone.

That earned me silence, at least for the time being.

"Yes, agreed," Persilla said, straightening. "They'll see reason where you lot are thinking with your hearts instead of your minds." She held up a finger to us. "Mind you, I will be there when they deliver their verdict. And if they want an arrow in her heart, I'll be the first to fire the shot."

I clenched my fists as a surge of anger ran through me, but Kaitsja's hand on my arm stopped me.

"Don't," she said softly. "She's just afraid."

She was right, of course. Persilla was only one voice in a chorus of fear, and no amount of arguing with her would change that.

They wanted reassurance and proof.

And they wouldn't believe Kaitsja was safe to be among us until an entire High Moon had passed—and even then, they'd never really trust her.

Generations of enslavement and abuse by the wolves couldn't be forgotten.

Yet, Daliah and her line had lived among the humans for generations. Their secret had been kept until now, and she had a plan to help them forget.

I just had to keep Kaitsja alive for a few weeks. I could have kept her in hiding. However, the plan I had concocted with her aunt required her to visit her sister.

Because her sister was dying, and only the Goddess could save her now.

If I let her sister die when I knew she could have been saved, Kaitsja would never have forgiven me.

And I would never be able to forgive myself.

"Come," I said, ignoring the villagers that were eyeing us with hunger. "Your sister needs you."

They wanted blood.

They thirsted for revenge, and I couldn't blame them. We lost a lot of good people last night.

Kaitsja's gaze filled with worry. "Is she all right?"

"She will be," I promised her. "But we need to hurry."

Because that was another thing Althea had told me. Her sister was to die during the Blood Moon.

She might already be gone.

But I had done something to buy her time. I just hoped for Kaitsja's sake that we weren't too late.

KATLYN

Every conflicting emotion I had was thrust out of my mind as I hurried toward the small hut I had always called home.

But was this still my home? Did I even *have* a home?

I certainly wasn't welcome here, and as much as Lyle seemed to be vouching for me, I highly doubted that the elders would side with him.

Hell, if I was in their shoes I wouldn't let me live, either.

But none of that mattered. I had started this journey in an effort to protect my family, and now my sister needed me.

Fires must have been burning during the night, because the stench of charred wood and grass assaulted my nose as I hurried to my childhood home.

It was so much smaller than I remembered it being. It took only a few strides to bypass the kitchen and small dining table to reach my sister's bedroom.

I paused in her doorway as I allowed my eyes to adjust

to the dim light. Her windows were boarded up with wood to shield against the storms, leaving only a single candle to reveal her bruised face.

Her eyes fluttered as she slept and her labored breathing seemed to shake the small bed frame. Dark lines bled over her skin, painting her veins black with the sickness that was slowly killing her.

"Luna," I said as I fell to my knees and gently took her frail hand in mine.

Cold. So cold.

I'd never seen her this bad before. "How long has she been like this?" I asked, not looking away. The dark lines had overtaken her entire body.

My mother answered from somewhere behind me. Lyle must have decided to wait outside, because I didn't sense anyone else in the small room. "Since last night," she said. "She's been asking for you."

The emotion was underneath my mother's words, likely threatening to destroy her. I knew her too well to buy the strong act she was putting on.

I'd learned so much from my mother and all I wanted to do was bury myself in her embrace and pretend none of this was happening.

But that's not how we had survived this long. She had taught me to face hardship, not run from it. She often went on expeditions alone to the southern lands in search of food.

We were survivors and we helped those who couldn't help themselves.

And that's exactly what I was going to do now.

Goddess, hear my plea, I whispered inside my mind.

Damn it all if I didn't have a literal goddess inside of me and I couldn't do something about this. I might value the humanity my mother taught me to uphold, but I wasn't human. Not really.

And I would fully use that to my advantage.

Where my body had accepted the wolf's magic, my sister didn't share that particular ability. What made me stronger made her sick.

The answers as to why that was frightened me, and I suspected my Aunt Daliah knew the answer to them.

Because, as Lyle had reminded me by using my secret name, she had called me Kaitsja my whole life.

That meant she knew something about my wolf.

The beast prowled in my soul. Her heat still made my temperature literally rise, but concern for my sister tempered her needs.

For now.

"I've always known you were different, Katlyn," my mother said from behind me. She rested a hand on my shoulder as we both watched Luna's chest rise and fall.

Her breathing was too shallow, too weak.

"I was afraid of it at first," she said. "I felt two souls in my belly when I was pregnant with you. I told myself I was going to have twins, but when you were born, my sister tried to tell me what you were. I just didn't want to hear it."

I stiffened at her mention of my Aunt Daliah. She never talked about her shunned sister, even if she did allow me to visit her.

"What did she say?" I asked.

My mother sighed as her touch disappeared. She

moved to the side of the bed and it tilted as she sat next to my sister. She brushed dark hair from Luna's eyes, gently tucking it behind one ear. Luna favored my mother in appearance, and had she not gotten sick, she would have been just as strong as her.

Maybe even more so.

I, on the other hand, favored my aunt, and now I suspected why.

"She said you inherited our family gift."

"Curse, you mean," I whispered.

The rumors had followed me all my life. Our family line was respected because of the female warriors it produced, but there were also those like Aunt Daliah.

Women who had gone insane.

But it was so much worse than that, wasn't it? There was a reason for the madness that ran in my blood.

I finally looked up at my mother, for the first time noticing the dark circles under her eyes and the tiredness that clung to her strong shoulders.

She'd had to bear this burden for so long.

"I don't care what it is," she whispered back as her eyes went glassy with tears. "If you can use it to save your sister, then that's all that matters."

I gave her a nod.

Saving Luna should be easy for a goddess, right?

I'd brought Charlie back from the dead, although it seemed it hadn't come without consequences. He had changed, but it wasn't in a bad way.

Whatever consequence there would be for saving Luna, I would pay it.

Closing my eyes, I wrapped both of my hands around Luna's icy fingers and willed my power to life.

Come on. I know you're in there.

The Goddess wouldn't wake, but her power was inside of me ripe for the taking.

And right now I was desperate enough to use it without her guidance.

My wolf snarled as my fingertips lit up with power and I began to push it into my sister.

Come on!

My mother went completely still as I worked, but she had retracted her hands so that she wasn't touching Luna.

Probably a wise move. I didn't know what this power would do to a human, but it was power that *I* controlled.

Heal her, I commanded it.

The power was sluggish as if it didn't want to leave my body, but *I* was in charge here. What was all of this for if I couldn't even use it to save my sister?

A snarl escaped me, one that I knew came from my wolf. My mother flinched, but the magic inside of me responded to the primal order.

It moved, sending silver bleeding through my veins until it seeped into my sister's hand marred with black illness.

Her entire body illuminated with a soft, silver glow and she finally took a deep breath.

"It's working," my mother said, her tone heavy with hope.

Luna's eyes flashed open and she stared straight at me.

She had green irises, like me. They looked better

against her dark hair, but right now moonlight was rushing in to dampen the color.

Making her look even sicker than she'd been before.

"Kat," she said, her voice raw.

"I'm here," I said and squeezed her hand tighter. My magic faltered, so I bit my lip, tasting blood as I renewed my focus. "Hang in there, okay?"

She smiled at me and it felt so good to see that look on her face.

When was the last time she had smiled?

Or been happy?

Before she'd gotten sick, I decided.

Then a shudder ran through her as she convulsed. She doubled over onto her side and coughed, releasing black sludge over the side of the bed.

"Luna!" my mother sobbed.

"It's just the sickness leaving her," I said, although this didn't feel right.

Luna held onto me as she trembled. Her lower lip quivered as her white-washed gaze found mine.

"Kat," she said again, this time her tone determined. "I don't have much time, so you need to listen to me, okay?"

She was younger than me, but not by much. Now she seemed to be the one trying to comfort me instead of the other way around. Gods, how had she matured so much in just the month I'd been gone?

"You have plenty of time," I insisted as my vision blurred with tears. I pressed her hand to my forehead and drew in a ragged breath. "You hear me? I'm going to burn this illness out of you!"

She whimpered as I pushed another wave of brutal power into her body.

"Kat," she said on a cry, forcing me to stop. I glanced up, only to find her trembling as dark lines snaked over her throat. She tugged at her thin nightdress, revealing a cluster that had formed over her heart. "For once in your damned life stop trying to fix everything and *listen* to me. *Please.*"

My lower lip trembled as I slowed the rush of power. "Luna."

She fell onto the bed, her breathing turning labored again. "I've known what was coming for a long time, Kat. Aunt Daliah explained it all to me."

My mother hissed at that information. "When? She knows she's not allowed in here or to—"

I gave her a look that sent her into silence.

Kat licked her lips and I reached for a cup of stale water on the small bedside table. I frowned at it, then redirected some of my magic to cleanse it.

At least that seemed to work. The foggy water cleared, allowing me to see through to the small scratches at the bottom of the wood.

I handed it to her and Luna took it with both hands, leaning over to gulp it down.

When she was done, she rested on her side. Pain seemed to roll through her in waves and it infuriated me that she had to go through this.

"Did Aunt Daliah say how I could help you?" I pressed.

Maybe I was just going at this too hard. She'd woken up, at least, so that had to be progress. Surely there was more I could do.

Her fingers trembled as she clawed at the bed, seemingly barely able to keep the pain at bay.

"Luna," I said, my voice firm. "You need to tell me what to do. I'll do whatever it takes. Do you understand?"

She closed her eyes, gasping for breath. When she finally spoke again, her voice was barely above a whisper. "There's nothing you can do, Kat. The illness is too far gone. But you can save the others."

My stomach dropped.

I refused to believe that.

"What do you mean?"

"Aunt Daliah told me about the cure. The one that can save everyone, but it requires knowledge of Calamity. She said—" Luna's information was broken off by a fit of coughs.

I held onto her as my mother fisted the bedsheets over her lap. "I think that's quite enough," my mother said. Her words were as cold as ice.

Luna ignored her and seemed to will herself into a moment of lucidity. "Unite them, Kat. End this war and all the corruption with it. Promise me, Kat."

The tears were flowing freely now and running down my cheeks. "I promise, Luna. Anything. Just please don't—"

A sob caught in my throat as Luna convulsed again. The moonlight I'd spilled into her seemed to damage her even worse than the darkness. Angry blisters formed where the silver had overtaken the black veins, making me panic.

"Katlyn, what did you do?" my mother bit off.

I shook my head, disbelieving that this was real. "I... I..."

Luna's horrible convulsions finally stopped.

And so did her breathing.

I stared at her for a long time as I tried to process the impossibility of what had just happened.

She can't.

No.

Luna!

My mind screamed. My wolf prowled, angry with no target to rip into.

Who was to blame for this?

My mother seemed to have the answer to that question. She leveled her gaze on me.

"Get out."

My heart was already shattered, but now the pieces twisted in my chest at her tone.

"Mom, I—"

"Get out!"

Devastated, I turned and fled.

Never in my life had I ever run from my problems, but this was too much to bear.

Lyle's waiting arms were there to grab me as I fell toward the dusty path outside my childhood home. He held me up when I would have fallen to the ground and never gotten up.

He led me away from the stares and the whispers. I didn't ask him where we were going.

I didn't care.

My sister was dead.

And it was all my fault.

KANE

Pain unlike anything I'd ever experienced ripped through my chest, forcing me to throw my head back and release an agonized howl.

Something terrible had happened.

Kaitsja!

I tried to call Her, but She was still blocking our connection. The wall between us seemed more solid than before, but even through the block I could feel the sharp stab of grief.

She'd just lost someone important to Her.

"Alpha?" Julian asked, concern lacing his voice.

While the others had returned to their packs to restore order, I was trying to get my wolf under control.

Or at least I was. Now he had fallen headfirst back into madness.

And I was right there with him.

I yanked against the thick chains spelled to keep me underground until the bloodlust passed. "I need to get to

Her," I growled, my voice more beast than human. "Free me, Julian."

"You ordered me not to remove these chains until that red ring around your iris dissipated," he reminded me.

That was an order I had made long ago if I ever fell into bloodlust again. Now, I regretted it.

He crossed his arms and leaned against the dungeon wall. "And you specifically said to disregard any orders to free you otherwise, including orders that came from you."

A snarl hissed through my lips as my teeth elongated. A shift threatened to descend upon me, something that was rare outside of the High Moon, but not impossible.

Certainly not when my mate was suffering.

I'll eat the beating heart of whoever hurt Her, I vowed.

"Kane," my second said, drawing my attention with the informal name. "You can't help anyone when you're too focused on eating hearts."

Huh. I must have said that part out loud.

"Something happened," I countered, working my mouth into words as I tried to reason with Julian. I strained against the enchanted silver. It dug into my wrists and burned my skin, twisted my bones as I pulled and tugged, but I didn't care.

I needed to go to Her!

Julian leaned in and I stilled, wondering if I'd gotten through to him.

"Orders are orders, *sir.*"

I snarled, then slashed at his scarless face, but my second had wisely remained out of reach of my powerful claws.

He was good at staying out of harm's way. That's what made him an adept second.

"Dammit, Julian! I finally found the Moon Guardian. My mate. My *Goddess*. Keeping me down here—"

"Is the best thing for her," he said, canting his head to the side. "You're not yourself, my alpha. You're no use to her until you're capable of leading the pack, much less *yourself*."

I growled, a low guttural sound that rumbled in my chest. The beast within me wanted out, wanted to rip the chains apart and tear into Julian for keeping me here and berating me.

But deep down, I knew he was right.

My mate needed me to be in control and right now I was an alpha in the throes of bloodlust. It hampered my reasoning and my ability to make logical decisions.

If I was free, no one was safe. I would kill anyone in my way, including those I cared about. The bloodlust had always been a potential problem, but this particular episode clung to me with claws dug deep into my psyche.

"But Kaitsja is—" I began, only to be cut off again.

"Is being watched, as you ordered," Julian reminded me. "Nina is keeping an eye on her through spy magic. She would have come to me if the Moon Guardian was truly in danger, but I'll confer with her and report back with an update, if it pleases you."

I took a deep breath, trying to reign in the animalistic rage that was coursing through me. I'd forgotten that I'd put in the contingency plan to have Nina magically spy on Kaitsja, but only if Her life was in danger.

The fact that I had forgotten such an important detail

only proved Julian's point. I was no use to anyone until I got my wolf under control, and I was barely hanging on to lucidity.

It was a miracle Julian had even managed to get me down here, but I vaguely remembered coming down willingly once the plan had been set in place.

The other alphas had left, gone to tend to their packs and they would be returning by day's end.

And my pack was in Julian's capable hands. Unlike the other clans, the Moon Pack ran smoothly with help from a hierarchy that had worked for us over the years.

Right now, though, I was regretting giving Julian so much power.

Mostly because I hated it when he was right.

"Fine," I grunted out, allowing some slack in my chains. "Report back to me as soon as you hear anything."

Julian nodded. "As you wish, Alpha."

He slipped out of the dungeon and sealed the door behind him.

It seemed my second wasn't going to leave anything to chance when it came to my wolf.

Something he'd learned the hard way. We all had. The last time I'd gone into bloodlust, I'd killed my brother.

My pack had never quite recovered from that, and nor did I. It wasn't something I often allowed myself to think about.

I clanked down against the unforgiving cold floor. Moon Blossoms grew in the corners, giving off soft silver light in the windowless room.

The irony wasn't lost on me. I'd kept the other alphas

down here for an entire month. The dungeon held their scents, and now they taunted me.

There was another scent that overpowered the alphas, and that was the floral fragrance given off by the Moon Blossoms. It reminded me of Kaitsja and the image of Her perfect face came to the forefront of my mind. Her memory was less of a taunt and more of an inspiration.

My wolf stilled when I thought of Her. He, too, desired Her. His rage was only because of his desire to protect Her, to Claim Her, and to keep Her from pain.

Her grief still soured inside my chest, but Julian was right. Her wounds were emotional ones, not physical, at least for the time being.

Whatever She was going through, I hated that I couldn't be there for Her, but I was going to have to do something that She deserved.

She was a Goddess after all, and She deserved my faith.

"I'll be there as soon as I can," I told Her, voicing my prayer aloud. "Hang on, Kaitsja. Remember who you are. Remember your strength, because without you, we are all doomed to carnage and darkness."

The Moon Blossoms brightened under my prayers, assuring me that Kaitsja heard my words.

So I closed my eyes and did the one thing my wolf couldn't do on his own.

I demonstrated patience and faith in our mate to find Her way, even without us to guide Her.

SHADOW

As much as I missed my territory, it felt good to be back in the main city. My wolf enjoyed the forest, but my human side appreciated more modern amenities.

I also had my own room that was dedicated to my line. I could have asked for an upgrade a few levels higher now that I was the Midnight Alpha—but I preferred this one.

It had everything I could need and wasn't obnoxiously large. Plus, the bed was enormous.

But even a warm shower and a whisky on the rocks couldn't improve my mood.

The humans had Katlyn, meaning that the Hunters still needed us.

And that was the only reason my pack was still alive.

"Alpha Shadow," Freas said from the doorway, holding a cell phone.

I glowered at him from underneath a curtain of damp hair, still not fully trusting the beta who had turned alpha.

It was why he used my name in conjunction with my title. There were more alphas than there ever had been before, and I had to take responsibility for playing a part in that.

It wasn't that long ago that the packs had suffered a massacre on a grand scale. We still didn't know who had struck.

The fingers had been pointed at each other, but now I suspected it had been the Hunters.

Regardless, I'd only just become alpha of my pack, as had Vern, Ryker, and Dash. This was a critical time for our packs and so far we weren't living up to our duty.

We'd left our wolves leaderless, and as a result, every pack had an awakening when the High Moon hit. Hundreds of alphas had emerged, all primed to take a role that they felt I and the other new alpha leaders weren't suited for.

Given how we had vanished for an entire month, I couldn't rightly blame them.

"Is it Vern?" I asked, hoping to hear an update from one of the other packs.

We were supposed to return to the Outcast mansion tonight, but I wasn't making much progress. I'd be staying in Crescent City or risk losing my pack for good.

"Actually, it's Alpha Kane's second," Freas replied, approaching me and holding out the phone. "He says he has an update only for the Midnight Pack Alpha."

He left the door open behind him, likely because he planned on retreating the moment I took the device.

"And that's me?" I asked, knowing the question was rhetorical, but my authority had already been challenged multiple times today.

Evident by Bjorn now locked up in one of the guest

rooms with spelled chains. I was no expert on Moon Magic, but the enchanted silver was still something most of us kept in supply for such occasions.

Freas wisely nodded. "Of course."

I hummed and took the phone, watching as the wolf retreated, not once showing me his back.

Smart wolf, that one.

I put Julian on speaker. Any wolf in the building would be able to hear him whether or not I turned up the volume. Wolf hearing was superb, especially in my pack. We were spies and trackers, best suited for stealth and espionage.

"I'm here," I said, knowing that Julian would recognize my voice. I'd been in his pack's house for a month's time and often made my opinion known, against my better judgment. Something about Kane rubbed me the wrong way and riled me up.

Although it was some consolation that the feeling was likely mutual.

"I have an update from Nina," Julian said.

I went quiet, knowing that Nina was a wolf in the Moon Pack with Hunter magic. She would have made a great addition to the Midnight Territories, given her ability to spy from incredible distances.

Despite the fact that it was the Hunter lineage in her that had started the Outcast war. That was one of many things I planned to change once I pulled my pack in order.

No matter how I felt about Kane, he was formidable and a wolf to be respected. He was the first alpha to recognize Katlyn for what she was: the Moon Guardian.

Our Goddess.

Our mate.

And I'd been doing my best to avoid thinking about her or else I would go mad.

"How is she?" I asked, speaking of Katlyn, not Nina.

Julian answered accordingly. "It seems that her sister has succumbed to the Moon Shadow Plague and her mother excommunicated her from the human encampment."

My muscles coiled at that information, both because I knew what it was like to lose a loved one. Logan had gotten me through that grief, but now Katlyn was alone.

"She needs someone with her," I said, already standing.

Fuck the Hunter agreement. The human encampment wasn't far and I could—

"She's not alone," Julian corrected me.

I squeezed the delicate device and it protested with a slight crack. "And who is with her?"

It better not be one of the damned alphas, especially Kane. Last I saw him he was still wallowing in bloodlust.

My mind didn't have a chance to spiral too far because Julian answered me. "The reborn human, Lyle. The one Althea told us about."

My teeth grated against one another, pricking my lips as they sharpened.

"You mean the one she killed?" I snapped.

"That is still not proven—" he began, but I cut him off with a snarl.

"Althea killed that human and you know it, or you're an idiot to think it was one of us."

It made sense to me and I'd started piecing it together within the past month. Dash had been out there with her in the woods, but he knew nothing of the human boy.

Which meant he didn't do it. Dash wasn't the devious type.

Katlyn had been motivated to infiltrate the city only because her human companion had been killed. And she hadn't done it alone. Guards were found dead with wolf marks on them, not arrows or blades. I knew of that little detail after listening to a debrief from Kane after he'd met with the other packs.

If it wasn't Dash, and it wasn't one of us, then it had to be someone from the outside.

The only other wolf out in that forest that night had been a white wolf.

And the only white wolf I knew besides Katlyn was Althea. There were other white wolves in the Moon Pack, I was sure, but none of them had been out there. I would have smelled them.

Every time something went down, Althea seemed to be at the center of it.

And now she had brought this human back to life using magic that didn't belong to her, all to continue to control the Goddess. Because he *had* been dead, I knew that much.

Kane didn't know where Althea was. Fuck, he was too busy trying to kill anyone in sight to make sense of who was where.

Julian refused to tell me anything, but my pack excelled in the trade of information. I'd already had spies return to tell me that the female white wolf wasn't in the Outcast mansion.

She was with the Hunters entertaining some meeting with another human.

I wondered if Julian knew that, but I wasn't about to reveal my sources.

I still didn't know who that human was at the Hunter meeting with Althea, but I did know it was a female. It was a matter of time before I figured out that puzzle.

"Regardless," Julian said, putting fake authority into his voice, "Althea is a member of the Moon Pack. She is our concern, not yours. I am only fulfilling my orders to keep you appraised of the Moon Guardian's whereabouts while Kane is otherwise occupied."

By otherwise occupied he meant chained up in a dungeon. That was the only realistic way to deal with an alpha high on bloodlust. It had to burn out of the system.

"Did you remove the Moon Blossoms?" I asked, knowing from first-hand experience there were plenty of magical blooms in there. That would only delay Kane's ability to leave his bloodlust. He needed to calm his wolf and tone down the magic, not amplify it.

"Of course," Julian said, not giving me any reason to disbelieve him.

But for some reason, I wasn't buying it.

"Good," I said, playing along. I'd go to the Outcast stronghold and sort this issue out later, but for now, Kane was going to have to get his shit together.

I had my own pack to worry about, and now our mate.

Because I didn't trust a human.

"About the meeting, I won't make it tonight, but I will be sending Freas in my stead." Not that I trusted the alpha, but at least Freas would look after the interests of our pack.

And a rebellion couldn't take place if I was in the city handling matters here.

"Understood," Julian said.

Then the line went dead. I growled, displeased by the subtle act of disrespect.

I was alpha here. I decided when a call was done.

But it didn't matter. I had a more prominent issue to take care of.

Kane's pack had Althea and Nina, but mine had a potion maker.

The phone rang and Hazel answered. "Yes?" she asked, her soft tones betraying her young age.

Her mother had been the potion-maker of our pack, and she was taking on the mantle after the massacre.

"Hello, Hazel," I said, turning my harsher alpha tones into a softer purr designed for pack members. "I have a favor to ask..."

KATLYN

An entire day had passed me by.

I vaguely remember Charlie taking me to my aunt's house after...

My mind wouldn't even form the words.

Not Charlie, my mind reiterated, choosing to focus on that instead. *Lyle.*

My eyelids felt heavy, but I forced them open because I feared what nightmares might await me if I truly fell asleep.

Images flashed through my mind like storyboards placed out of order, but my mother's voice was still vivid.

Get out!

Those words rang inside my head on a loop. It was a memory I would never forget. It was bad enough losing my sister, but it seemed that I had lost my mother, too.

It wasn't fair. I hadn't chosen to be born with a *curse.*

A feverish chill had overtaken my body, some sort of illness that had set in after I'd lost Luna.

Aunt Daliah might know what's going on...

But she wasn't here. My aunt must not have been home since the small hut was empty and quiet aside from a crackling fire.

My fists clenched the blankets at my chest as I lay on my side, staring into the flames. I was almost close enough to burn, but I always liked to rest like this in front of the small hearth.

My body felt cold and hot at the same time, causing me to shiver.

Lyle was somewhere behind me working on food. The only reason I knew that was because the scents of herbs and spices tickled my nose.

Nausea wound through my stomach, retaliating at the idea of putting anything inside my mouth.

My wolf wanted to eat, though. She clawed underneath my skin as if she wanted out.

Her idea of a good meal was something raw. Something that had to be chased and killed.

Blood, she begged.

She wanted to hunt, but that was her second choice to what she really wanted right now.

Which was sex. Given that the only male in my vicinity was Lyle, that so wasn't happening.

Not because the idea didn't appeal to me. But rather because it *did*.

The fever growing inside my body had something to do with my wolf's heat, and it was only getting worse, not better.

He wants you, my wolf insisted, but I ignored her.

I still didn't know if the attraction between Lyle and I was fabricated by my wolf's heat, some side-effect of bringing him back to life, or just a desperate attempt to forget my pain.

He did not deserve to be used as a shield against my grief.

"You need to eat something," Lyle said as he knelt.

My gaze flinched from the bright flame and I made the mistake of looking up into his face. He'd never looked more beautiful as the fire bathed him in golden light, clarifying his sharp jawline and kissable lips.

His forest-speckled eyes held so much emotion in them.

Concern. Worry.

Something else.

I curled the blankets up to my chin and forced myself to turn away. "I'm not hungry," I said, although my words only came out as a ragged whisper.

He set the bowl of soup aside and pressed the back of his hand to my forehead. "You're burning up, Kaitsja."

My stomach twisted when he used my name, and not in a bad way. "Please don't call me that," I begged.

Because I was riding a thin line of restraint right now. I'd already asked him to kiss me. If he got too close, I'd ask him to do so much more.

He nodded, then sat and rested his arms on his knees. "Do you want to talk about it?"

"Not really," I replied.

I wasn't sure if he meant my sister, what happened with my mom, or the fact that my wolf's heat was literally burning me up.

But I felt so cold at the same time, giving me an irresistible urge to squirm closer to the fire.

He chuckled. "If you get much closer you're going to climb in, and your aunt is going to make fun of my cooking skills again when I offer her seared Goddess."

A laugh escaped me, surprising me, and I clamped my jaw shut against the sound.

It didn't feel right to laugh right now.

"Do you know when she'll be back?" I asked instead.

He hummed. "It might be a day or two. She was with the Hunter groups working on negotiations."

That sounded... interesting.

But it also meant we were likely going to be stuck here for a while. I wasn't sure how I felt about that.

"Lyle?" I asked after we'd fallen into a moment of silence.

"Hmm?"

I bit my lip, then decided my request wasn't out of line, if anything, just to keep the nightmares away.

"Can you hold me while I fall asleep?"

He went still for a moment, and I wondered if I'd asked too much.

But then I felt his hand on my hip. His warmth came up from behind me as he brought a pillow and settled in.

"Anything, Kaitsja."

I bit my lip, because I'd asked him not to call me that.

Regardless, I liked it, and with his comfort pressing against my spine, I finally closed my eyes.

The nightmares didn't find me.

But something else certainly did...

SHADOW

It was difficult to wait until midnight to use the potion, but Hazel told me the efficacy of it had to do with the moon's position.

So I would wait, because Katlyn needed me tonight and I was determined to be there for her.

But I didn't expect to feel like a pup waiting on his first run with a female. Because that's exactly what this felt like.

Katlyn was in heat, and while that was not something I was going to take advantage of, it would allow me to ease her pain when it came to her grief.

The bottle was cold in my hands and I turned it with my fingers, examining the diamond glittery substance inside.

Moon nectar, she'd called it.

Rare.

Precious.

And very, very valuable. Only the Midnight Pack had

retained the wisdom of its creation from our ancestors. I doubted even the Outcasts knew how to make it.

At least, I prayed they didn't. Because then I might not be the only one paying Katlyn a visit tonight.

I'd moved to the balcony overlooking the city.

Sky rises towered high, a testament to what humanity used to be before the wolves took over.

Before we nearly wiped them out.

I never had really agreed with the historical accounting of how humanity had been suppressed. Wolf shifters were part human, after all. As superior as the alphas had always made wolves out to be, it was something I often questioned.

Silently, of course.

Sure, it was the storms that seemed to do the most damage. Wolves could handle the magical rains, but it made humans sick.

Most of them, anyway.

But where had the storms come from? Why did no one seem to question that?

After the things I'd learned so far, it felt like I'd only started to peel back the layers of the truth.

I pondered everything I thought I knew as I took in the stretch of night over the quiet city. It wasn't like the wolves to be still, but grief hung over the territories like a blanket.

The sky was clear, revealing a sprinkle of stars visible even through the light fog of this area. It was a Valiance Pack ordinance to keep every building at a limited lumen level because wolves needed the moon, even here in such high rises.

Moonlight glimmered over clean windows. This city was maintained by all of the packs so that we could share the connection to our Goddess, but the largest population was from the Valiance wolves. They were political types, best suited to be in a position of neutrality between the various territories and the hub of the Crescent Moon.

What good that did us.

I was far from home. My lands rested to the east closer to the ocean where our boats could travel and explore what was left of this world. Shadow Territory got its name from the inhospitable darkness from which it came.

It was why my fur was black. I had the least exposure to the vibrancy of our moon throughout my life.

Which made me most sensitive to it. Even though the moon was on a waning cycle, its magic rippled over my skin everywhere it touched like electricity.

The potion in my grip felt like bottled ice—so cold it burned.

"Almost there," I said to the night sky as the moon climbed. A sliver of darkness kept it from being a High Moon, but it was more than enough magic for me to work with.

When it hit an invisible precipice, I popped open the cork.

And drank the sweet contents, relishing as the honeyed nectar glided down my throat.

And set my soul on fire.

KATLYN

"Hello?" I asked into the dark.

This was a nightmare, a fever dream, or I was just losing my mind.

Shadows stretched out everywhere, but my skin was alive with silver ice.

Rainbow sequins glimmered in my footsteps and followed my fingertips as I moved.

It was disorienting, to say the least, as I split the gloom with my approach.

"Who's there?" I asked, using my fingers to stretch the darkness apart like a curtain. I winced when a stab of pain ran through my stomach, but I ignored it.

My wolf's heat wasn't going away any time soon, but I was growing accustomed to the pain.

And adrenaline was keeping me focused, for the time being.

I expected to find someone waiting for me on the other side of the shadow curtain, but I only found more of the black nothingness.

"I know you're there," I tried again.

Because I wasn't alone in this strange place that smelled like Moon Blossoms and midnight.

A growl emanated from somewhere far away, making me double over with a hiss of pain.

My wolf reacted to the sound, the sensation as if she'd just jabbed her claws through my chest.

She seemed to lift her attention inside my soul, perking her ears at the welcome noise. Because that growl was designed for a mate.

One of my alphas was here, wherever *here* was.

"I guess we go this way," I said to my wolf, knowing she was too far gone to reply to me as I forced myself to straighten.

Her heat was driving her mad, and if this kept up, she might rip me in two trying to get out. I didn't understand it and I didn't know how any of this worked.

I desperately wished I had someone to explain it to me, but my aunt wasn't home and I couldn't return to the wolves. The first alpha to find me would try to claim me, High Moon or not. I had no doubt about that, because my heat was still in full force.

No, going back to the wolves wasn't an option.

I wasn't sure I even wanted to after everything that had happened.

Yet, I found myself drawn to the growl that rumbled through the dark landscape, leading me across invisible stretches of dreamscape that seemed to surpass vast distances.

My legs burned by the time I reached him and my wolf was prowling inside my head.

He was nothing but a shadowed silhouette, dark against dark.

But all that changed when I approached.

Darkness bled away to reveal his beautiful face, making my stomach flip for an entirely new reason. Shadow, the Alpha of the Midnight Pack, was aptly named.

He seemed at home here.

The scar down his eye seemed less angry tonight, as if he had time to heal. His black silky hair had been combed and neatly draped over his eyes.

I'd ventured close enough to peer into them, wondering how I had never noticed how his dark eyes were speckled with diamonds as if he held the skies above within his soul.

"Hello, Shadow," I said, unable to resist going on my tiptoes, reaching up to brush away his loose strands of his hair to get a better look at his face.

He leaned into the touch, bending down so I didn't have to strain. "Little wolf," he replied. "I was beginning to wonder if you could even find me."

His words still held the heavy rumble of his growl, but I liked it. The sound calmed me and made me feel at ease.

My wolf preened at the noise, temporarily pleased by this level of contact.

It was strange. I'd never been at home with a growling beast, yet here I was, petting him like he was a beloved pet.

Reluctantly, I withdrew my fingers and forced myself to break eye contact.

Then regretted it, because everything had changed while I'd been fascinated by the male.

"Where… are we?" I asked, taking in the incredibly beautiful room.

I'd never seen anything like it.

A bed large enough to fit my entire family.

Lights that didn't use fire.

Perfect walls with lavender shades of color.

My bare feet brushed against an endless soft rug as I explored the room. My toes curled into what must have been the largest sheep to exist—but wool didn't feel like this.

I'd only seen things like this when…

When I went to the Epicenter.

The wolf city.

"This is one of the suites reserved for visiting alphas," he explained, as if any of that meant something to me.

"Uh… huh," I said, wandering to a built-in table by the wall that had drinks on a serving tray.

I picked up one of the perfectly transparent glasses, and then opened a bin that had ice in it.

Oh gods. Ice!

I drew out one of the cubes and held it between my fingers for a moment before drawing it into my mouth.

I groaned.

"Little wolf," Shadow warned.

I jumped, because his voice had come from right behind me. I turned, then looked up because he wasn't leaning down this time.

My jaw worked on the small cube, crunching it when I

wanted to savor it. But Shadow was looking at me like there was something important to discuss, and the ice in my mouth was melting too fast anyway.

One of his hands went to my hip, freezing me in place.

Because I liked his touch.

My wolf seemed to come alive in the moment, making me bite down on the remainder of ice as I groaned against the pain. My skin prickled as if she ran her claws along my insides, and a howl resounded inside my mind, making me grab my temples.

"Your heat is worse than I thought," Shadow said, his tone strained.

I fell into his chest. He wasn't wearing a shirt, but he was wearing pants.

"Are you going to… fix it?" I asked him, not sure what answer I was hoping for.

Because this had to be a dream. Sex with a made-up version of my alpha couldn't hurt things, right?

And maybe it would take the edge off.

"This isn't a dream, little wolf," he said as if he could read my thoughts.

I curled my fingers against his chest, lightly scratching him in the process. "It's not?"

He certainly felt real.

But none of this made any sense. I shook my head, trying to remember.

Unpleasant memories surfaced in response.

My sister.

Luna.

Then my mother…

Get out!

A whimper escaped me as the memories tossed themselves at me in broken pieces, cutting through me like shards of glass.

Shadow still had his hand on my hip, keeping me steady. But now his other hand curled through my hair to the roots of my scalp as he tucked me in close. "Shh," he said, accompanying his words with another low growl. "I know you've been through a lot. You don't have to talk about it, but know that I've lost someone I love before, too. And I wouldn't wish that grief on anyone." He lightly tugged on my hair, forcing me to look up at him. "But you're not alone like I was, okay? I'm here for you little wolf, however you need me. I can just hold you like this all night until the moon sets. Then you'll go home, and if you want, I'll summon you again."

My throat worked on a swallow. "Summon me?"

He lightly scratched his nails against my scalp, relaxing me. "Yes. There's a potion that can call the Moon Goddess, although I wasn't sure what would happen in this circumstance. It seems that it brought your spirit to me, just for tonight."

My eyes widened.

So... this wasn't a dream.

I would have backed away, but Shadow had me locked in his grip. Perhaps the confinement wasn't intentional, because a moment ago I was about to fall, but with one hand on my hip and another threaded through my hair, I was entirely under his control.

"Shadow," I said as my wolf snarled inside my chest. "Let me go."

She was growing impatient. She wanted me to do things with this alpha that wasn't right.

He tried to kill us! I reminded her, but she either couldn't hear me, or didn't care.

Desire pooled low in my stomach and my thighs clenched.

Shadow's nostrils flared, warning me that his superior senses definitely picked up on how I was feeling.

Lust clouded his eyes, but he did as I requested and released me.

The lack of his steady grip sent me stumbling back until I reached the dresser. I curled my fingers over the edge as I gulped in a deep lungful of air.

"Why did you summon me?" I asked, already knowing the answer.

He wanted what all alphas did. He wanted to take what didn't belong to him, to devour and—

"Because I sensed your pain," he said, interrupting my thoughts with words that didn't match my narrative.

I glanced up at him, curious now that his muscles rippled with self-control.

He'd backed away from me and now sat on the bed. He'd placed a pillow over his lap, likely to hide his erection.

Everything about him seemed tense and coiled as if ready to strike.

Yet he wasn't. Why?

"Why do you care about my pain?" I asked, wanting to keep him talking.

I felt like I was learning something about this wolf. This was the first time I'd had true one-on-one with one of the alphas that had rejected me and chased me down like a dog.

Yet he'd groveled and shown his regret, just like all of them had when Kane claimed me in front of them.

The memory of Kane's unique form of passion made desire flare again, making my entire body tremble.

Shadow's nostrils flared in response as his gaze flicked down. He seemed to force it up again to look into my eyes. "I don't deserve for you to forgive me, or believe me, but I do care about you, little wolf. I made a mistake, one I can't take back. But what I can do is help you in any form that might take."

I bit my lip and thought about that.

He had undoubtedly worked with Kane for a month on how to rescue me from the Hunter's Hell. I could argue that was for selfish reasons, yet if he truly wanted to take me as his mate without my consent, he would have done so by now.

I was primed, weak, and my wolf prowled in my mind, her claws raking underneath my skin with a demand to give in to this alpha's comfort.

Her heat was nearly unbearable. My temperature spiked and my entire body burned with fever. It was unlike any sickness I'd ever experienced, considering I didn't feel ill.

I felt alive.

Hungry.

"You said you lost someone," I replied, wanting to start there.

I didn't want to talk about Luna, but maybe hearing his story would help.

Because I felt responsible. We'd been out in the storms because of me, because I had miscalculated the wind and how fast the storms should have traveled that night.

And I failed to save her even though I was supposed to be a goddess now.

My own mother had cast me out. So had my village.

If I wanted them to forgive me, accept me, I needed to first figure out how to forgive myself.

And maybe... that process started with an alpha like Shadow.

He nodded. "Yes, a close friend of mine." He tilted his head. "In some ways, she had been a little sister to me."

That captured my interest. I slipped down the edge of the dresser to sit on the floor. "What happened to her?"

His jaw flexed. He fisted the pillow before responding. "She was murdered."

My eyes rounded. "Oh." I didn't know what to say to that.

Shadow's expression had turned dark, making me wonder if the murderer was still alive. "You have to understand, the packs have devolved through the generations. I suspect the Moon Goddess did her best, but the evil present in our kind is why the storms exist." He leveled his gaze on me, something powerful settling between us. "You're the Moon Guardian. You're the Goddess incarnate. I made a mistake rejecting you, Katlyn. Because you're the only one who can fix this fucked up mess. The wolves need you." He sighed, releasing a low growl that made my stomach curl in response. "*I* need you, and I'm sorry I didn't see that sooner."

I doubted Shadow had ever used so many words in consecutive order, much less admit that he *needed* someone.

Needed *me*.

Instinct guided me as I moved to the bed and perched on the end. He remained still when I rested a hand on his arm.

Electricity jolted between us, making me suck in a breath, but I didn't pull away.

I was starting to learn the real person behind the wolf, and that changed everything.

Maybe I wasn't ready to forgive him, but perhaps I could understand him.

"Althea said that the storms existed to find me," I told him, hoping that might be some small measure of comfort. "So if you're blaming yourself for the darkness in this world, please don't."

His gaze lifted to meet mine. I was surprised to find hurt there. "Damn. How do you do that?"

I canted my head to the side. "Do what?"

He ran his fingers over mine, seeming to indulge in the sensation.

I allowed it, for now.

"Make me *feel*."

"We all have feelings," I responded. There wasn't anything special about me, so I wasn't about to take responsibility for making his heart beat.

It was my wolf doing that. The Goddess inside of me, not *me*. Not really.

He continued to stroke my fingers, taking his time to

linger on each one. "Not a member of the Midnight Pack, little wolf. That was beaten out of me at a young age. When I watched children killed right in front of me, all for the purity of the bloodlines in our pack, I shut down. I did the easy thing and turned it all off." His fingers ran up my arm until he cupped my face. "You somehow have a key to a box I locked a long time ago." His gaze flicked from one eye to the other, as if he was trying to memorize my face. "One that has my heart inside."

I couldn't help it. The draw to him was too strong.

I leaned in and brushed my lips against his.

He froze, allowing me to explore with my tongue, learning the soft notes of coffee and chocolate as I licked his lower lip.

Shadow was a mixture of bitter and sweet decadence, and I couldn't bring myself to resist having a taste.

"Tell me what you want, little wolf," he said against my mouth. He still hadn't moved a muscle, but his fist was pressing against the pillow seemingly to keep it in place.

"I want my beast to stop clawing at me from the inside." It amazed me I didn't have bleeding wounds running down my arms by now. "But I can't give her what she wants." I glanced up into his eyes, taking in the tension between us until I felt like I was going to snap. "I have to know it's real, not just some magical, fabricated reality because my wolf demands it."

He nodded knowingly, as if that made total sense to him. "You wish for courtship."

I paused as I considered that word.

Courtship.

Yes, that made sense. I didn't want to just dive into bed with the alphas of all five packs because of "destiny." As far as I understood it, I had been mated to these alphas because of circumstance.

I could choose to have them replaced, if I so wished. Evident by the fact that hundreds of alphas had appeared on the night of the High Moon.

Because Shadow and the others weren't qualified?

Because I deserved superior mates who hadn't tried to kill me?

I wasn't so sure if that was really the reason. My wolf suggested that it was their absence from their packs and the heavy influx of Moon Magic that had spurred the emergence of contending alphas—not because they weren't qualified. Fate had a role to play in that. It was not coincidence that I had mated all of them at once.

Fate or not, I decided my destiny. If my alphas were the answer to solving this world's problems, I could learn to love them.

But I had to be sure. My wolf agreed with putting them through a test, at least. She wanted a show of blood and strength in the woods, but we hadn't been able to stick around long enough to see that happen.

So a different sort of test was in order.

What better way to truly test their worth than through courtship?

"We do this my way," I said finally, talking more to my wolf than to the alpha watching me.

"Your way," Shadow agreed, remaining unmoving while my lips still hovered over his.

I would test this alpha's resolve.

I would test his capacity for restraint and boundaries.

Because my wolf's demand for reprieve couldn't be ignored, but we could both get what we needed if Shadow was willing to compromise.

Time to play, my alpha.

Time to kneel.

SHADOW

I clamped the pillow onto my rigid cock as Katlyn slowly explored my skin with her tongue.

Each lick was slow, deliberate, and seemed to quell the animal inside of her.

Her skin burned as if she was on fire, and I knew that the heat was consuming her.

Her control and restraint were impressive, to say the least. I wasn't trapped in the rut, so I had my senses about me, but my wolf absolutely reacted to Katlyn's siren call.

She'd begun releasing a little purr of her own, granted I wasn't sure she was aware she was doing it. The adorable rumble went straight to my dick, making it pulse underneath the pressure of the bedding.

"Fuck," I cursed when she licked behind my ear, seeming to enjoy punishing me with her sensual teasing.

"We won't be doing that," she vowed.

I wasn't sure if she was trying to convince herself, or me.

"No fucking," I reiterated, disappointed, but not surprised.

She wanted to be courted, and I fully intended to do that.

But there was only one way to help her through her heat. She would come to learn that the hard way, it seemed.

"May I touch you?" I asked, knowing that every liberty required permission.

"Not yet," she said, continuing to explore me. "Stand up."

My beast enjoyed this authoritative side of her.

Although, there was a weakness and insecurity beyond a wall. The only reason I recognized that was because I was very good at building walls.

I'd always thought that my upbringing had destroyed my capacity to feel, but that couldn't be further from the truth. Something that was irrefutable when one private conversation with this little wolf opened up so many things inside of me.

Like my need to claim. *That one* I suppressed with all the skills I had learned over the years in restraint and control.

I did as she ordered, slowly rising to my feet and allowing the pillow to fall.

Katlyn didn't hide her interest in my arousal. She walked in a slow circle around me, trailing her fingers over my chest while she did so.

"You're beautiful, Shadow."

Her praise made a rumble roll through my chest. I knew my growls would affect her, but my control had its limits. "As are you," I said, unable to keep my eyes off of her.

She was wearing human battle leathers and they fit her to perfection. Her top neatly formed a "V" toward her belly button, while her pants hugged her ass, giving me an unimpeded view of her curved shapes.

I would need to take those off of her to accomplish my goal.

"You're burning up," I informed her. "You should take those leathers off."

She gave me a wry smile. "Should I?"

Growling in response, I leaned in to encourage her compliance.

I would respect her boundaries, but my wolf needed a taste, or I was going to go mad by her scent alone.

Her fragrance of jasmine and moonlight awakened my animal.

But it was a third scent that captured my interest. When she leaned into me, pillowing her breasts against my chest, a delicious musk of *woman* made me snarl.

Because she not only called to my beast. She awakened the man inside of me as well.

"Use your words, Alpha," she chided, although she'd pressed herself against me as I rumbled my warning.

"Take your clothes off or I'm going to use my teeth," I warned her.

Was my patience wearing thin? Maybe.

She would just have to deal with it.

"Use your teeth, then," she challenged as she swept her fingers down my abdomen.

I grabbed her wrist before she could go any lower. My restraint only worked if she didn't touch me *there*.

I would be touching *her*. That was how this night would go.

She squealed as I flipped her onto the bed and my canines sharpened. I wasted no time ripping into the thick leathers, then peeled them away.

I took her shirt off first, revealing rosy buds that begged to be licked.

So I did, and was rewarded when she hissed in a breath as she bowed off the bed.

I pressed one hand on her abdomen to keep her in place as I continued my mission.

"Stay," I ordered.

She growled in response.

I growled louder.

Then I used my teeth on the fabric at her hip, stripping it open with a sharp yank.

Three more bites and the fabric was free, revealing supple skin underneath.

She pressed her thighs together, but I pushed them open, and groaned at such a beautiful sight.

"You're so wet, little wolf," I praised her, then ran one finger over her pussy. It easily slid inside, finding her center.

I enjoyed her blazing heat, so I added another finger.

"*Shadow*," she warned as her muscles clenched around me.

"*Stay*," I ordered again as I lowered over her.

Her fragrance was intoxicating.

This is heaven itself, I decided when I ran my tongue over her, rewarded when she bucked and cried out.

I kept her in place with my other hand still firmly placed on her flat stomach.

She had tormented me, and now I would return the favor.

She whimpered when I licked again, this time with a little more force, so I pulled away and looked up at her.

"Do you wish me to stop, little wolf?"

She was so fucking beautiful as she gazed down at me over the mounds of her plump breasts. Her lips parted on a pant as she widened her legs for me, arching herself at a better angle. "Don't stop," she protested. "Please, gods, don't stop."

I rather liked the sound of her begging. Of her saying *please*.

So I pulled out my fingers, licked them clean, and spread her.

Her legs had started to tremble and I could feel her eyes on me, watching my every movement.

So I swirled my tongue around her clit, then closed my mouth over it, and did the same motion again.

She moaned, clearly enjoying my technique.

I wondered how much experience she'd had before, because I could tell she was no virgin—something that might bother Ryker. Only because he had withheld for the sake of respecting the Goddess.

Which was absolute bullshit. Sex was a primal act, one that honored our deity.

"Tell me what you like," I said, my breath on her wet

heat. "Do you prefer this?" I swirled my tongue, then lightly nipped her sensitive bud, earning a jolt from her. "Or this?" I asked, then more gently grazed my tongue up, then down.

"I need..." She bit her lip.

I pulled away in reprimand. "What do you need?" Communication was vitally important in a courtship. I would not make the mistake of hurting her simply because I assumed.

Assumptions had nearly ruined everything.

I'd assumed Katlyn had been an imposter, that she had killed the Goddess and that destiny had made a mistake.

How wrong I'd been.

Had I killed Katlyn that night because of my own ignorance, I would be no better than the broken members of my pack.

Her cheeks flushed an adorable shade of pink as she seemed to build the courage to answer. "I need... more."

Oh, more I could do.

"As you wish, little wolf," I said, then closed my mouth over her.

And began to growl.

She screamed, but I was ready and I kept her pinned in place with my hand on her.

My other one slipped beneath and cupped her from the inside.

I needed to feel her body to know if I was too rough.

This woman was like a fine instrument, one I needed to learn to play properly.

And oh, I would make her body sing for me.

Her inner muscles quivered, telling me that she could

take more. If she had been overly tense, I would have stopped.

But she was giving into the pleasure.

"Such a good girl," I murmured on her sex, then suctioned my mouth over her and released a heavier growl.

One that continued on a long rumble, vibrating her center.

She panted as she pulsed around me.

My cock throbbed and my wolf snarled, ready to plunge inside of her.

But I held him back by the scruff, reminding him who was in control. We would court our mate, earn her trust, and pay our penance.

Slick gushed from her and I lapped it up, intoxicated by the sweet essence.

Omegas were a rarity, and I had never had the pleasure of tasting the floral nectar. It reminded me of the potion I had used to summon her, but it was so much sweeter.

And the impact went straight to my cock, making me edge a climax of my own simply from the effect.

This was what it was like to pleasure a goddess, and I was determined not to disappoint her.

I licked and thrust my fingers in tandem, upping my growl to a heavy rumble, vibrating the sound over her swollen flesh.

She twisted as if she was trying to get away from me, but she was such a good little wolf, voicing her needs. "Don't stop," she begged. "I'm going to—I'm—"

I clamped down on her in tandem with a hard thrust of my fingers, rewarded by her explosion in my mouth.

She screamed as her inner walls clenched around me.

I couldn't fucking wait until she did that on my cock.

My growl maintained, only decreasing in rumble after I had fully seen her through her first orgasm.

"Gods," she breathed, sagging against the bed. She moved her thighs to close her legs, but I would not be deprived of her sweet pussy.

I was only just getting started.

"You're still burning up," I informed her as I ran my fingers down her slick heat. "We're doing that again until your fever breaks."

She blinked at me with incomprehension.

Oh, she'd never experienced a wolf before.

"Again?" she asked.

"Mmm," I agreed. "I'm not some human boy, Katlyn. I'm a wolf, and I'm going to devour you whole."

She opened her beautiful lips to protest, but I had already shoved my tongue inside of her.

She had said no fucking, but I decided my tongue didn't count.

Her fingers threaded through my hair as I did it again. She threw her head back with resign.

"Why do you have to be so good at that?" she asked, groaning when I licked her from the inside.

I spread her wider, shoving in deeper, and kept going until she couldn't use her words anymore.

As I made it my mission to make her come on my mouth again.

But not before I added a little pain to her pleasure. It would only increase her sensation.

She complained when I pulled out, but then froze when I teased my sharpened teeth over her delicate skin on the inside of her thigh.

I wanted to mark.

I wanted to *claim*.

While fucking her was off the table, she hadn't said anything about biting.

"I'm going to bite you, little wolf," I said, looking at her for confirmation. "I need you to tell me if this is something you want."

I would not draw blood without her consent.

She stared at me for a moment, then ever so slightly, her head bobbed.

"Words," I growled, skimming her thigh with my teeth.

"Y-Yes," she stammered. "I want that."

I grinned.

Then sank my teeth into her flesh, eliciting a scream from my little wolf that would be heard from the heavens and back.

With my mark in place, I went to work with my fingers, making her come on my hand, next with my mouth, and afterwards I flipped her over, and started it all over again.

LYLE

Fury raged through me as I gripped the windowsill and stared at the light drizzle outside.

I'd been holding her, as she requested, until she'd fallen asleep.

And then her dreams had started.

Now I had moved as far away from her as possible, or else I was going to go mad.

So here I was, staring at the weather outside that better represented my current mood.

Dark and angry.

It wasn't the kind of storm that would give humans plague. After a High Moon there was usually a small reprieve in that regard.

But I couldn't leave, not until I knew Katlyn was okay.

She moaned in her sleep, clearly having a vivid dream of the sensual sort.

Sometimes she screamed.

And just now, she'd cried out with such force I had

thought something was wrong—until she started to beg for more.

Indecision rooted me to the creaky wooden floor. A part of me wanted to leave, but another part knew she was burning with fever.

She was sick and I couldn't leave her.

"Shadow," she breathed.

The name made me see stars. She kept saying it, over and over again.

And I knew she was dreaming of *him*. One of her alphas.

Althea had told me of her mating to the alpha of each pack. Something about her destiny to unite the wolves.

I didn't give two shits about wolf politics, much less uniting them.

In fact, it was the infighting between the wolves that gave humans a chance. If they quelled their differences, then what was left of humanity would finally be wiped out.

The last remaining human village had been more or less left alone simply because we weren't worth the trouble. The wolves had other things taking their attention—like rivalries and pack politics.

Humans weren't worth their time.

Until now, anyway.

With the alliance of Hunters and humans, wolves realized that we weren't completely helpless. We could fight back, if given a chance.

Which put a target on our backs.

Katlyn made a sound again, one that stirred powerful emotions inside of me.

This was pure agony.

Cursing, I went back to her, because I wasn't one to give up on Katlyn, not after everything we'd been through.

The damp rag I'd placed on her head needed replacing. I knelt and took it off, then dunked it into a bowl of cool water.

Her cheeks were flushed and her lips parted as her dreams consumed her.

And what a dream it must be.

Her fingers clenched into the furs I'd put around her, because despite her temperature, she shivered as if freezing.

I placed the cloth on her forehead again and frowned as it steamed.

She was literally burning up. How long was this damned wolf heat supposed to last?

"Hang in there, Kaitsja," I said, using the old nickname for her. Then again, it wasn't just a name that had stuck around from childhood.

It was the name of her wolf—her hidden identity.

According to Daliah, she was more of a hybrid than a true wolf shifter, although she had been born with a wolf's spirit inside of her. The way her aunt had explained it to me was that her wolf had been dormant until enough magic awakened it.

I'd noticed something different about my childhood crush early on.

She was too fast. Too strong.

She picked up scents and sounds better than any

hunter I had ever seen—although she thought she hid that about herself.

And then she'd survived the storms unscathed when her sister had grown ill. She'd claimed to have abandoned Luna and saved herself, but I knew that wouldn't have been true.

She would never have left Luna alone in a storm.

I had seen right through it.

And I'd never said a damn word, because I knew what would happen if the others knew she wasn't fully human.

They would turn her away, and that's exactly what happened.

Anger bubbled up inside of me. It was something I had hoped to be wrong about. With the Hunters here, things were different. There was hope in the air.

Not just hope—anger.

Too many wanted revenge. Too many wanted blood.

That's why Daliah was with the Hunters right now trying to negotiate some sort of peace between the races. She thought that her niece would be the glue to pull everyone together—Hunters, humans, and wolves.

It was a nice fairytale.

I had agreed to care for Kaitsja until Daliah's return and get her niece through her heat, even knowing what that might entail. I wasn't a wolf, so there wasn't much good I could do even if she asked it of me.

Which made this so much worse.

Her lips parted on a moan, her dream reaching a fever pitch.

It felt wrong to watch her, but she was so damn beautiful. I wanted to be the one to make her sound like that. I wanted my name to be the one on her lips.

As always, it was my damn sense of duty that helped me see reason.

Kaitsja wasn't mine.

She never had been.

I was her protector. While I didn't agree with her aunt's plan for her, I knew she would change the world. She only had to be given a chance to do so.

She never listened to the rules.

She never followed the path destiny had paved for her —she'd always carved her own.

I pressed my hand on the cloth that had already bled through with her heat. "Hang in there, Kaitsja," I told her, knowing she couldn't hear me, but I would comfort her anyway.

It would take her about an hour to burn through the wet cloth I'd just put on her, so it was a good time to patrol before the sun came up.

Grabbing my weapon's belt and bow from the corner of the room, I set out to hunt us a meal. There wouldn't be much game out there after the High Moon, but this area had seen some reprieve in the past month.

There was even a restored creek out back suitable for drinking and bathing—a surprise I intended to show Kaitsja when she woke. I was so grateful for a bath that I didn't even question Daliah when she told me she'd used a little magic to bring it back to life.

I could definitely use a *cold* bath, as it were. Assuming Katlyn slept through the night.

And if she slept, that was just as well, she most likely

needed it. Perhaps I could wash off before she got up, then I could patrol the area again while she took her turn.

She continued to make whimpers and needy sounds as I gathered my things and paused at the door.

Her brows creased as if she was in pain, but I knew women also made that face when approaching an orgasm. While I'd never been intimate with Kaitsja, I'd gone through a romantic phase.

Mostly in reply to her escapades. It had been an effort to get my mind off of what she was doing with the other eligible young men in the village.

I'd never had the courage to tell her how I really felt.

At least, *Charlie* never had the courage.

As Lyle, though, it was all I could do not to jolt her awake and kiss her until she made those sounds just for me.

Shaking my head, I turned away. "Sweet dreams, my flower. I'll see you soon."

And then I left the hut, not stopping until the music of the forest overtook Kaitsja's screams.

KATLYN

My throat was raw by the time I finally woke.

"Ugh," I groaned as I rolled onto my side, finding the fireplace reduced to embers.

A dry cloth fell from my forehead and I stared at it for a minute, feeling disoriented.

Memories came to me in broken fragments. Luna's death. My mother casting me out.

Things that should have made me want to throw the furs over my head and not wake up for days, yet I didn't feel that way at all.

I felt… good. And that made guilt rise its ugly head.

Frowning, I tried to make sense of it. What had happened next?

That's right, I'd come to my aunt's hut with Lyle.

A quick perusal of the room showed me he wasn't here, but that wasn't cause for alarm. As hunting partners, we often took turns patrolling.

And I had emotions to deal with right now, as muted as they might be. My stomach still churned with grief and

I sat up and rubbed my eyes. I wasn't ready to face those feelings, not yet. But there was something that had dampened my sorrow.

I swiped a hand over my face, finding it... cooled.

"Wolf?" I asked, curious if she felt any different.

She stirred, but huffed at me as if she was still sleeping.

She felt... sated. For now.

My fever had broken during the night and I was definitely better. Although, a frown tugged at my lips. I was forgetting something.

My fingers went to my throat, finding it raw.

Then my eyes went wide.

Shadow...

That had been a dream, right?

The contented waves of pleasure humming through my body suggested it had either been a very, very vivid dream, or all of it had been real.

A throbbing sensation on the inside of my thigh caught my attention, so I stood and shimmied out of my leathers.

I stared at the bite mark and ran my fingers over the healing ridges.

Real, I decided.

It was mind-boggling to realize that I'd been spiritually teleported through my dreams to another place, with an alpha who had summoned me.

And bitten me, it seemed.

The mark didn't look like it was going to heal completely, and I knew that would please Shadow immensely. He'd passed my test. I'd established a boundary that he could not claim me, yet he'd still found a way to show his intent to any who might see it.

Blowing out a breath, I fixed my pants and found my bow leaning against the wall.

The sun was up, meaning Lyle would probably be returning soon if he'd gone out on a dawn route. So I decided I would meet him partway.

Too many emotions were vying for my attention, and when things felt overwhelming, action was what suited me best.

My stomach rumbled with hunger. My last decent meal had been my feast as a wolf on the night of the High Moon that had been more replenishing than nourishing. It was time to find something to keep up my strength. I knew better than to expect this lull to last very long.

Whether it be humans, Hunters, or wolves, someone would be coming for me eventually.

So I grabbed my things and headed out to do one of my favorite things in the world.

The hunt.

Triumph swelled in my chest when I found not only two rabbits, but a pheasant, as well.

We were going to eat good tonight.

My stomach was momentarily content, thanks to the berries I'd found along the path. There was so much more life than before, and it gave me hope that things might finally be improving.

Whistling, I had my bounty slung over my shoulder as I approached the hut. I hadn't run into Lyle, but it was entirely possible he was avoiding me. His firewood and earthy scent had always been unmistakable.

The entire forest smelled like him, and not just because those scents complimented the trees. His marker was distinct, one that invited comfort and companionship.

It was in part why I had never pursued anything romantic with him. In fact, I'd tried to forget about him with many flings, none of which seemed to fully work.

Because I would always return to him and venture out on long hunts together. I would stare at him in the night and wonder if he ever thought of me in that way.

Of course not. I was like a sister to him, or at least, that's what I had always thought.

Now, I wondered if I'd gotten it all wrong.

Pausing at the hut, I listened to the sounds of splashing water which were unexpected, to say the least.

The wind was heading north, though, so I would have scented bodies of water during my patrol.

Setting down my kills at the front door, I ventured behind the hut only to be shocked at the massive creek that most definitely hadn't been there before.

It wasn't just the creek that stunned me, but the row of Moon Blossoms at the creek's edge framing the very naked male inside of it.

Lyle was turned away from me, his broad back on full display.

I couldn't help but take in the sight, my eyes tracing

the lines of his muscles and the way water droplets clung to his skin.

Had he always been that muscular? Because damn.

"I thought that wolves were more your type," he said without turning around.

I flinched and suppressed a curse. *Of course he heard me coming.*

Lyle was a hunter, a survivor, just like me, and very little got past him.

"You just caught me off guard," I said, forcing myself to turn around.

Water splashed from behind me, suggesting that Lyle was getting out.

His clothes must have been somewhere on the bank, as well as some furs, because he took his time drying off and getting dressed.

"There didn't used to be a creek here," I said, desperate for some sort of conversation that wouldn't point out the obvious.

I had been definitely staring.

Because wolves weren't necessarily my type—survivors were.

Shadow had survived a horrid upbringing and everything that had happened since.

Lyle and I had come from caring homes, but we'd suffered far too much death and disease not to learn how to survive.

"Or wild Moon Blossoms," Lyle agreed, referring to my comment about the creek. Rocks crunched underneath his bare feet as he approached.

Assuming he was dressed, I turned around, and then blushed.

Because he was only wearing pants and the front of his body was just as manly as the back. He even had those nice little dimples by his hips that seemed to be made for tongues to trace. And either he'd stuffed a sock in his pants or…

Lyle cleared his throat, forcing me to look up. "Do you want to talk about it?"

I blinked at him a few times. "Talk about what?"

His forest-speckled eyes seemed to drag the truth out of me, whether I wanted to talk or not. "Your night with Shadow."

That wasn't what I'd expected him to say.

Oh gods, did I make sounds in my sleep?

I decided to play dumb, because that always worked so well for me. "Who's Shadow?"

He huffed a laugh. "Look, Kaitsja. If you don't want to talk to me about it, that's fine, but don't treat me like I'm an idiotic little boy who follows you around like a lap dog you like to keep on a leash. Because I'm not that boy anymore."

His anger seemed to slap me right in the face and I stared at him as he huffed and brushed past me, muttering something about extra furs if I wanted to bathe.

I flinched when the door to the hut slammed, indicating I was very much alone.

Irritation flared in my chest as I ripped off my hunting leathers and kicked off my boots.

What kind of rise did he get by treating me that way?

A part of me wanted to follow him in that hut and give

him a piece of my mind, but his reaction didn't make sense.

"When did I ever treat you like a lap dog?" I pondered as I slipped into the cool waters.

I would have enjoyed it. The feeling of this place was reminiscent of the magical area I'd found surrounded by Hunter traps.

There wasn't as much magic here, but it explained some of the restoration in this area.

I wonder if my aunt had something to do with this.

More questions were starting to pile up for her eventual return, so I hoped that she didn't take too long. Lyle had said she was working on negotiations with the Hunters, whatever that meant.

As I lathered with a cube of goat soap Lyle had left for me, his words rolled over in my mind.

The only reason I had been attracted to him was because of my heat, and I didn't want a fake relationship.

But what if I was wrong about that? Lyle had changed, not just in his name but nearly everything else about him.

His body, his demeanor, and the way he spoke to me. All of it was different.

Maybe our relationship would naturally be different, too.

"What does it mean?" I sighed, laying flat in the water as I stared up into the sky.

Perhaps there was something between us and his anger was just jealousy. He'd definitely heard me say Shadow's name in my sleep, which meant... I wasn't even sure what it meant.

My heart was starting to split in different directions and I wasn't sure what to do about it.

Kane had immediately grabbed onto me and made his intentions known. His complete devotion and worship was hard to believe, but it was genuine.

And Shadow was so much more complex than I'd initially realized. I was working on forgiving him, because when I stepped back and looked at the bigger picture, I couldn't blame him for reacting the way that he did.

And if I could find a way to forgive Shadow, then the others deserved a second chance, too.

I wasn't sure where that left Lyle, but I knew I had to talk to him.

Because if there was something between us, then shouldn't that come first?

He'd always protected me and been there for me.

Even now, he looked after me while I cried out another man's name.

I really need to talk to him.

With a sigh, I left the creek. Glimmers of silver followed me as if there was a hint of Moon Magic still alive in the water.

Or maybe it was alive in me.

Warm furs met my damp skin as I wrapped up in them. My leathers needed washing too and I scrubbed them before hanging them on limbs to dry.

Clutching the furs to my chest, I ventured back to the hut. My kills were missing, but I smelled them cooking from inside.

My mouth instantly watered and my wolf perked up.

Meat? she asked, eager for a real meal.

"First we talk to Lyle," I told her. As much as I wanted to stuff my face, I was going to be in this hut with my hunting companion for a while yet, and we couldn't dance around each other as if nothing was happening.

When I ventured inside, I found Lyle sitting by a revived fire, his face twisted in pain. He clutched his arm as his jaw flexed.

"What happened?" I asked, rushing over to him. "Are you okay?"

He glanced up at me, then looked away as if embarrassed. "Cut myself while skinning the second rabbit." The first was cooking on the fire, while the second was mostly skinned and resting in a bowl.

"Let me see," I ordered. He removed the soaked rag, revealing a nasty gash wound over his right wrist, which was still bleeding.

"Give it here," I said, letting my furs hang on my body where I'd tucked them. They'd be secure enough not to fall, probably.

Lyle didn't protest when I took his hand and examined the wound. Of course he'd cut it deep and hadn't cleaned it properly at all.

"This is how you get an infection," I chided. And it wouldn't have been the first time he'd been clumsy with a knife and gotten himself into trouble.

He silently watched me as I worked. I was familiar with the process. I warmed a bowl of water on the fire, and gathered some fresh cloths as well as healing ointments my aunt had stored on the shelves.

She'd taught me how to make them on my own, so I always had a stash of them in my room or in my emergency bag. Neither of which I'd had access to for a while, so it was nice to have her resources.

As much as my mother had seemed determined to keep my aunt out of my life, I'd spent most of my spare time in this hut.

Lyle hissed when I poured cleaning ointment on the wound, but he stayed still, which was all that I needed from him.

Once I was done, I took off the cooked rabbit from the fireplace pike and set up the second one. Then I set out two plates and divvied up the first rabbit.

I placed the pheasant in the small root cellar to keep cool until we were ready to treat it.

Then we quietly ate until every delicious morsel was gone.

"You're always so good at that," Lyle said, breaking the silence after I'd cleaned up the remains and washed my hands.

"At what? Making sure you don't die of rot instead of a wolf bite?" I snapped, then pinched my lips.

Because he *had* died from a wolf's attack.

"Sorry," I amended. "That was uncalled for."

He grabbed my hand and lured me to the floor by the fireplace. "I'm being a jerk, so I think I deserved that," he said, his voice pitched low. "And I meant that you're good at fixing things... Fixing *me*."

I huffed and looked away, but his hand was still holding mine. "I don't know. It seems all I've accomplished was to start a new war. That's why my aunt is with the Hunters, right? To negotiate a truce after I mucked everything up?"

His fingers trailed up my arm and curled into the roots of my hair. His nails lightly scratched, the sensation reminiscent of how Shadow had comforted me the night before.

Fresh desire curled in my stomach and my wolf began to prowl.

My temperature started to rise sending my skin prickling with fire.

It seemed my heat was back.

Fuck, not now!

"What I said was wrong, Kaitsja. You didn't treat me like an idiotic little boy; I *was* an idiotic little boy. I idolized you and put you up on a pedestal, but never told you how I really felt."

I stared up at him, stunned by his bluntness. "What do you mean?"

None of this made any sense.

Or maybe it made *too much* sense.

He leaned in and brushed his nose against my cheek, making my heart pound in my chest. "I mean that I've always loved you, Kaitsja. I still do. And I want you more than I want to breathe. Hearing you dream about *him* last night killed me, and I'm sorry for taking it out on you." He brushed his lips over my skin, eliciting a tremble from my body. "Gods, you're burning up again. And there's not a damn thing I can do about it."

I was panting now. My fingers curled into the loose furs hanging around my chest and part of me didn't care if I ripped them off.

A secret part of me had always wanted to hear these words.

But now everything was so much more complicated.

"It wasn't a dream," I said, knowing I had to be truthful. Even if I hurt him, I was tired of dancing around our feelings for one another. I leaned away so I could look into his eyes. Brown orbs speckled with green watched me with the same intensity that I felt. "Shadow used Moon Magic to summon my spirit to him, and he was... helping me."

Lyle seemed to process that. "And did it help?"

I made a fist, amazed that the furs hadn't disintegrated by how hard I clenched them. "Yes. I think so. My fever broke for a few hours."

But now it was back with a vengeance.

Daggers sliced through my lower abdomen and need clawed through my skin. My wolf prowled and purred, demanding reprieve from the growing pain.

It seemed to be coming on stronger than before. Whatever Shadow had done had only been a temporary fix.

But regardless, Shadow *had* given me a reprieve. Even if I couldn't seek a resolution to my heat, I could appease it, for the time being.

"Then let me help," Lyle said, shocking me to my core.

"But, that's not fair to you," I said. It was an honest response. Not only would I be asking something incredibly intimate of him—but I also couldn't promise him exclusivity.

He'd just told me he loved me.

But how could I say the same in return? Those feelings were absolutely there. They always had been in one form or another, but I certainly couldn't act on them.

Shadow would likely summon me again, and when he did, I wouldn't be able to resist him.

I wasn't human anymore. I was part wolf, and Shadow was an alpha that called to the primal parts of me.

It was a call I was going to have to eventually answer.

"I don't care," Lyle said. He held my wrist so hard he cut off the blood flow. The needles tingling through my fingers were a small sensation compared to the roaring flames igniting in my core. "I said I'd do anything you asked of me, Kaitsja. I meant it." He released me, only to turn his iron grip on my furs. "Let me help you, or send me away. Those are your choices, because I'm done pretending there's nothing between us. I'm not that boy anymore."

I didn't move when he pulled the furs and spread them neatly away from my body.

But when he lifted his hand to touch me, I pushed him away.

"No, Lyle. That's not how you help me."

Hunger had returned, and since I hadn't satisfied it with Shadow, it had come back two-fold.

I knew what I needed, and it was something even Shadow hadn't earned.

But Lyle certainly had.

Disappointment crossed his features, but he immediately stood as if to leave.

I stopped him by gripping the waistband of his pants.

With a pull of ties, I undid them and slowly tugged the cloth over his legs. "You help me by letting me apologize for ignoring you all these years. Because I was the one

177

who made a mistake, and you're going to let me try and make up for it."

"Kaitsja," he protested, but I knelt in front of him and readjusted my furs on the ground. They pooled around me as I took in his impressive size and length.

Beautiful.

He opened his mouth to say something again, but I silenced him with ease, by raking my tongue along his shaft.

Because this hunger would only be sated by taking what I needed.

And right now, I needed Lyle. I needed to apologize.

I needed to feel his love, and acceptance. And perhaps, somewhere along the way, I'd rediscover my own.

KATLYN

I knew how to please a man, but it was different with Lyle.

Perhaps it was my heat and my reinvigorated hunger, but once I tasted him, I couldn't stop.

A crazed need overcame me as I grabbed him with both hands and took him as far as I could down my throat.

He'd backed against the wall and seemed to restrain himself as I sucked and licked, my arousal growing with every pulse his dick made for me, every groan that left his mouth.

"Slow down, little flower," he told me, and I paused with my tongue grazing the sweet precum budding on the head of his cock.

My eyes rolled, because *yum*.

A man had never tasted like this to me. Usually it was a little sour, or didn't taste like much at all. But Lyle was honey and ecstasy. Every taste made me more crazed.

You're welcome, my wolf purred.

Little beast. She knew how to make a man's come taste like a treat *and* it was an aphrodisiac to my senses. No wonder I was desperate to taste Shadow.

"I think this is making it worse," Lyle said, somehow sounding lucid when all I wanted to do was climb him like a tree.

He pressed a hand to my forehead, but that's not where I wanted his touch.

"You're too hot," he said, his voice laced with concern now.

A growl ripped from my throat. I stood and tried to grab him, but he spun me, pinning my arms above my head as he held me in place by the weight of his hips.

I was painfully aware there was nothing to separate us, and his hot arousal seared my belly.

I squirmed, desperate to place him where I wanted him.

"Speak to me, Kaitsja," he demanded.

He reminded me of Shadow at that moment. *What is with these males and their words?*

But that's where the similarities ended, because Shadow had worked his magic tongue and made me scream. Lyle wasn't touching me at all, and wasn't letting me touch him—that's why my heat was worsening.

When I couldn't free myself, a whimper escaped me.

What was wrong with me?

"Shh," Lyle said, closing the gap between our lips. He kissed me once, making my body wilt in submission. "I'm going to help you, little flower. Be a good girl and spread those legs for me."

I didn't want a repeat of what Shadow had done. Lyle

wasn't my servant or a *lap dog*, and I had intended to prove that.

Yet I found myself obeying when he pushed his knee between my legs. His thigh gave me exquisite pressure on my throbbing core, and I whimpered again.

"More, please," I said, desperate as I soaked his leg in seconds. His pants were open, giving me access to his cock, but I hadn't taken off his clothes completely.

He shushed me again with his mouth, then nipped my lower lip.

A growl rumbled in my chest, but my wolf had certainly liked that.

He kissed the column of my throat, then moved down to kiss his way over my chest.

Forcing me to endure sweet agony, he took his time as he rolled his tongue over my left nipple. He sucked, then released me with a pop.

He laved the other side, then finally continued his path south.

My fingers curled through his hair as he kissed my belly button. He couldn't seem to resist rolling his tongue inside the divot—something I wanted to do on those dimples at his hips.

It tickled, then he wrapped his hand around my thigh and opened me only to—

He paused, staring.

I looked down, wondering what had his attention.

Then realized he was staring at the bite mark Shadow had given me.

He ran one finger over the healing wound. There definitely must have been Moon Magic in the creek, because it had almost fully scarred over, leaving a pink line behind in the shape of Shadow's sharp teeth.

"When did this happen?" he asked.

A lie lingered on my lips. I could have told him it happened a month ago at the last High Moon, or that it was from the time Kane claimed me when I wished to punish the alphas who rejected me.

But I wasn't going to lie to him anymore. I wasn't going to lie to myself.

"Last night," I said, hating how he pulled away from me as if recoiling. "Shadow asked me if he could bite, and I said yes."

His forest-speckled eyes flashed upward. "You *told* him to do that to you?"

A shiver ran up my spine in response to his anger. He was still intimately close to me, and had a full view of how aroused I was.

"Yes," I said, my voice just barely above a whisper.

I shrank back when he launched to his feet, now towering over me.

Had he always been so tall... and intimidating?

If he had been a wolf, his growl would have put me on my knees. The sound he released was just as primal, and had me pinching my legs in need. "I thought he was just *helping you* last night."

I whimpered when he palmed my sex. His fingers were confident and rough. Nothing like the Charlie I remembered. This was all Lyle.

And I liked it.

"He was."

He continued ruthless strokes, his fingers slipping through my wetness with ease. "Did he help you like this?"

I whimpered when he thrust two fingers inside, not even bothering to prime me.

Not that I needed priming. My body had changed and right now it was made for sex.

"Yes," I whispered, ashamed when I widened my legs for him.

Because I needed so much more than his fingers, but I would take any reprieve right now.

My stomach burned, my skin tingled, and my body was on fire. I feared I would combust if Lyle didn't give me what I craved.

"You seem like you're not satisfied," Lyle said as he leaned in, roughly shoving another finger inside. "Did he fuck you?"

"No," I answered honestly.

"Why not?"

I swallowed as his fingers paused, four of them filling me up. I knew he could feel my walls pulsating around him as my wetness dripped from me, desperate for more.

But the answer to his question wasn't a simple one. I forced my brain to connect the dots.

"Because he tried to kill me. Because he has to court me and earn his place at my side to amend his mistakes. Because he's an alpha, and I don't just want a wolf. I want a man."

There, I said it.

Lyle curled his fingers, touching a deliciously sensitive part inside of me. "Lucky for you, I'm all man."

Yes, yes he was.

"I want you," I said honestly, but quickly added, "and I want Shadow, and Kane. Perhaps even Vern, Dash, and Ryker as well. I'm connected to all of them, Lyle. I'm not human. Magic has bound me to them and that's not going to change because you want it to."

It wasn't as simple as a magical bond, but rather what I hoped I could accomplish with their help.

And if I admitted it to myself, what I'd seen in Shadow surprised me. There was more to him than I had first imagined.

He could complete me in no way anyone ever had. And if Shadow made me feel that way, I knew better than to judge the others without first really getting to know them.

I wasn't sure where Lyle fit in the picture—but I knew I wanted him, too. I wasn't going to deny that.

His jealousy burned almost as hot as my heat. I could see the fires in his eyes, and I briefly wondered if that's what gave him his ember scent that was so alluring.

"Then you have me," he said after a moment. He rolled his thumb over my clit, making me squirm.

"But you're jealous," I said. It was obvious.

"I am," he agreed. He surprised me by removing his fingers, and then he positioned himself at my entrance.

I froze, and my breath hitched in anticipation.

"But if you want me, if you care for me, that will be enough, Kaitsja. Say the word, and all I have is yours."

I swallowed past the lump in my throat. "I more than care for you," I whispered as I lowered myself, desperate to feel him inside of me. "I love you, Lyle." I swallowed again. "And I want you to fuck me."

He didn't wait.

He didn't hold back.

He thrust into me, completely sheathing himself inside of me as I screamed.

I wrapped my legs around his hips as he drove into me against the wall, bruising my back against the hard stone of the hut's interior, but I didn't care.

"More," I demanded. He growled as he thrust into me with brutal strokes, making me cry out as I raked my nails down his back.

It was so fucking good.

So much better than any of my so-called flings. For the life of me, I couldn't remember why I hadn't considered Lyle first.

I knew why. I didn't want to destroy our friendship.

More than that... I didn't want to hurt him, because he was too good for me.

I must have said that last part out loud, because he flipped me, pressing my breasts into the stone that felt like ice against my heated breasts.

He slammed into me from behind, then stayed there, leaving his throbbing cock deep inside my body. "You think I'm too good for you?" He snaked his hand down and palmed my clit, circling it until my legs started to shake. "Maybe that's true, because you're all I can think about, little flower. And it makes me want to murder knowing a wolf made you come first." He kept up his ruthless circles, forcing me toward an orgasmic edge. "I'm going to make you come for every time I had to hear you say his name. I'm going to squeeze pleasure out of you until you are begging me to stop."

When his strokes rushed me toward a brutal climax, I tried to force my legs closed, but he wouldn't let me move.

He pressed his hips against me and settled in as deep as he could go, keeping me in position as he swirled my clit with his fingers. "Come for me, little flower. Be a good girl for me."

I'd started to whimper as I clawed against the stone, but there was no escaping the intense orgasm he intended for me.

My muscles spasmed as I reached the cliff, and then I fell off head-first into sweet, decadent oblivion. My legs shook and Lyle pressed down hard in time with the pulse of my body.

I knew now why he was buried so deep inside of me. He could *feel* my climax, and he could match it with his movements.

It only drew out the pleasure longer, draining me of all my energy as I slumped against the wall, completely spent.

When the spasms finally stopped, he slipped out of me and my wetness splattered onto the floor.

With the wolves, I wasn't embarrassed about it. They knew what I was, but Lyle was human.

He took my arm before I fell. His bandaged wrist was at my hip, but the majority of my weight he took on his good arm.

"I'm sorry," I said, not sure exactly what I was apologizing for.

Making a mess all over the floor?

Losing control?

Admitting to him that I wanted the alphas who had tried to reject me?

I'd said that he was too good for me. I still believed it.

Because none of this changed the inevitable. My alphas would find me again, and I would go with them.

Even after this. Even after experiencing heaven with Lyle.

Tears rolled down my face, and that seemed to surprise him. "No, I'm sorry, Kaitsja. My jealousy is getting the better of me." He guided me to the pile of furs in front of the fire.

Our poor second rabbit was burned to a crisp by now, so he gently set it aside.

"Let me try this again," he said, this time rolling me on my back and he slipped between my legs.

And then he kissed me as he entered me again, amazing me with his stamina.

Maybe coming back to life had given him a little bit of virility from Moon Magic, or maybe he was just that grounded in self-control.

Because he fucked me for hours, giving and never taking.

Going slow, gentle, and doing exactly what he promised. Drawing out orgasm after orgasm until I was completely spent, and fell asleep in his arms.

RYKER

Unease had me wound into a tight knot all day. It wasn't just the fact that my wolf still wasn't talking to me.

I was closer to the Goddess than most, and something most definitely was going on with her.

We should be out there looking for Katlyn. Not here holding hands with the enemy while the storms raged through southern territories.

"This is a waste of time," I growled, my voice only loud enough for Vern at my side.

Vern didn't disagree with me, but he didn't reply either as he remained stoic in his position at the corner of the room while the meeting slowly progressed.

If I wasn't alpha of my pack, I would have left. But I couldn't. Not when it was my responsibility to make sure tonight didn't end in a bloodbath.

We were in neutral territory. One of the outposts used by my pack, the Mercury Mystics, was the natural choice when it came to the unprecedented meeting between the

This was a historical moment. Hunters, humans, and wolves had congregated here in my territory.

And right now, a Hunter was having it out with a human woman. She was the only reason I hadn't dismissed this so-called meeting.

Because she was supposedly a blood relative to my mate.

"Kaitsja was almost killed," she growled. Had she been a wolf, it would have been a more impressive sound. Regardless, the woman certainly had an air of authority about her. Unfortunately, that wasn't the first thing I'd noticed that made her unusual.

Madness tinged her eyes and she seemed pained when she moved.

I knew what it was. I'd seen that hollow look before in shifters. There was a type of defect that appeared and made a shifter crazed.

But that only happened to one who was born without the other half of his or her soul—without a *wolf*.

It was a strange phenomenon, one that we hadn't yet worked out the cause for. We didn't see it very often, and if a pup was born without a beast in their soul, it was often put out of its misery.

"She has a Corrupted deity within her," the Hunter replied. "I did what I thought I had to do."

I snarled. Vern placed a hand on my arm for the third time tonight.

I didn't understand how he could just sit here and listen to this blasphemy. Despite this so-called *truce*, the Hunter still defended his actions to kill our mate.

"We agreed to let them hash it out," Vern reminded me. "Logan reasoned with him. Now, let this take its course."

I glowered, but my gaze shifted to the wolf he mentioned.

Only Shadow knew the strange shifter, and he wasn't here. Which put us at a disadvantage. We were playing this game blind, and I was going to let Shadow know my feelings about that when I saw him again.

Either a punch to the face, or maybe a second scar down his eye.

Whatever he was doing, it couldn't be that important while our mate was out there under the protection of a single human.

Ridiculous.

A rolling rumble vibrated in my chest. My reply for Vern was thick with sarcasm. "Right. The Hunter is going to stop his pursuit of our Goddess after bringing his entire legion across realms to take her out. All because his *boyfriend* said so."

Logan's piercing blue eyes held a steady gaze on mine. It was a challenging stare, one that would end in blood with most alphas.

But the strange wolf wasn't from this realm. He could have been challenging me, or he was simply watching me.

That's what I didn't like about him. He was too mysterious—too unpredictable.

And he was apparently in a mate-circle relationship with the Hunter, which made all of this even more fucked up.

He crossed dicks with the Hunter and got him to lay

off long enough for a truce, and I was supposed to be grateful?

I swiped a hand over my face. "We could really use Shadow." I wasn't sure why he wasn't here. He had given some vague excuse having to do with establishing the hierarchy of his pack.

He wasn't the only alpha among us struggling with that. Alphas had emerged throughout all of the packs in response to our absence, but it didn't change the presence of the Hunters and our need to deal with them.

Shadow had even ordered his pack to return to the city as soon as possible. A move I understood, yet didn't agree with.

We needed to stick together.

As much as I hated to admit it, we were all starting to work better as a unit. Maybe it was because most of us hadn't been alphas for very long, or maybe it was because we'd all mated the Goddess and now naturally worked better together.

I even missed Kane's arrogant input—not that I'd say that out loud.

"We have Freas," Vern offered, indicating the newly emerged alpha with a nod.

I glowered at the dark-haired male that was smaller than Shadow, but looked just as mean with his bushy brows and bulky stature.

Except he was fucking useless. His only interest was kissing Shadow's ass and getting back into his good graces. That was evident every time he opened his mouth. Apparently Shadow thought Freas was vying for control of the Midnight Pack, but it had been another wolf named Bjorn to be the real problem.

All updates I'd received second-hand from Julian of the Outcast Pack after being informed of Katlyn's situation.

It was a wild tale, one that involved bringing some human companion of hers back to life, while she lost her sister to a plague caused by the storms. And then her own family had cast her out, meaning she was alone with a single human to guard her.

If my wolf had been talking to me, I would have felt him desperate to find her, to comfort her, to *claim* her.

I'd made a horrible mistake rejecting her and the only thing I wanted to do was try and make up for it.

Perhaps I could never earn forgiveness, but I could spend the rest of my very long life trying.

"This is a waste of time," the female named Daliah snarled, capturing my attention.

"See?" I whispered to Vern. "She agrees."

Vern rolled his eyes.

He might have made a retort, but the female had turned to the group of wolves, leaving her back to the Hunters.

Brave—or stupid.

She stood and the jingle of her bracelets reminded me of tree limbs rattling in the wind. "What say you lot?" she asked, staring directly at me, then at Vern and finally Dash. "Are you just going to wait around until the Hunters find where I've hidden my niece?"

"Hidden?" Dante said, standing. His hand had gone to the blade at his hip—one he refused to part with even when we'd explained the rules that there were to be no weapons in a truce meeting.

He'd countered that we all *were* weapons, so it was even. Not exactly something I could argue with and decidedly let that slide.

Now I was regretting it, because I did not like being threatened in my own house.

"Yes, hidden," the woman said, spinning on the Hunter.

The female had a damn death wish.

Except, she'd started to glow.

And what's that floral scent?

"She's using Moon Magic," Dash said, having approached my right side while Vern took the left.

"She is," Vern agreed.

My fingers curled into fists. It was starting to get really fucking annoying that my wolf still hadn't resurfaced.

He expected me to do this on my own.

You made the problem. Now you fix it.

His sentiment rolled around in my head like an unwanted voice.

The row of Hunters behind Dante stood—one of them taller than the rest. His general's name had escaped me, but I knew he was a monster to contend with.

Hell. They all were.

Logan was the one to step between the human and the Hunters now holding their blades. "Enough," he snarled, putting his beast's growl into the word. He held up his hands as he spoke. "You all agreed to a truce. Do you know the definition of a truce?"

Dante glowered at him. "She's hiding the Goddess

from us. No matter her fate, she cannot be allowed to wander this realm as Calamity approaches."

Calamity was a word I recognized only because Kane had caught us up to speed during the month we had searched for our mate.

It was another realm's problem, one that insisted on bleeding into ours.

"There is no Calamity here," I snapped, fucking tired of this shit.

Vern reached out to stop me, but I waved him off as I faced the Hunter.

"That is a magic from *your* realm, not this one," I growled. "So why don't you just go back where you came from and leave us alone? Take Calamity with you."

Even if I didn't have my wolf with me, I was naturally tall, so I was able to match the Hunter's height.

It didn't make him any less intimidating, but I was an alpha—I wasn't easily intimidated.

And I was done being jerked around by the Hunters.

Dante took his time staring me down—one alpha to another.

He might not have been a wolf, but he most certainly was an alpha, nonetheless.

"Calamity doesn't differentiate between realms, Ryker," he said, using my name as if he fucking knew me.

I snarled, not appreciating his familiarity. "Neither do Hunters, it seems."

He shared a look at Logan, then seemed to relax as he released his blade. "You're wrong. I've decided to respect your realm and do everything in my power to cleanse it, but I need the cooperation of your people to do that." He glanced at the fuming human female. "*All* of your people. Logan has convinced me to give you time to figure it out."

She scoffed as her fingertips glowed with silver. A giddy madness lingered in her eyes and her speech took on a strange accent. "Then you're going to be waiting forever, Hunter. The beasts are never going to put their dicks away long enough to see reason." Before I could react to the insult, she stabbed a finger at the Hunter. "And you have a short memory, beast-killer."

That was an odd thing to say, but the woman was clearly missing a few sticks in her bonfire.

Dante's expression changed, though, suggesting her words had hit a sensitive spot. "If you have gone through what I have, none of you would be dismissing Calamity so quickly." He shoved his blade back into its sheath, the sound making the woman flinch. His burning gaze swept over the group, finally lingering on me. "I give you all until the next High Moon to hand over the Goddess. We will investigate a different way to cleanse her before resorting to death." He glanced at Logan. "But death is what must happen if all options are exhausted and she remains Corrupted. We cannot allow the disease to spread. We have seen what it can do and it is worse than any of you could ever imagine."

"Worse than decapitating a Hunter in front of his generals?" I suggested, earning a gasp from the crowd.

"Ryker," Vern hissed.

I frowned. It wasn't like I started the threats.

And this was my territory. I would not tolerate such behavior, especially when this was supposed to be a truce.

Dante simply glowered. "You have until the next High

Moon. Then the truce ends," he said, his words low and deadly.

With those final words he turned and left, his Hunters following behind him.

Logan rested a hand on my shoulder. "I'll talk to him," he promised.

"You do that," I growled.

Logan had done all he could to keep the Hunter at bay. That much was evident.

We had less than a month to get our act together.

Logan gave me a nod, then left.

"It's time to pay Shadow a visit," I said, earning agreement from Vern.

"I'll go with you," Dash said.

I gave him a nod, genuinely appreciating that. The Soldier Alpha would be an excellent resource while venturing into Crescent City.

"Then you both go while I settle things here," Vern said. I could tell he wished to come too, but he would act as my second in my territory. Even though he was the alpha of the rival pack, I trusted him with my life. It had always been that way between us.

He'd do what needed to be done. He had a level head and had been raised with political leanings—even if he hadn't been raised to be an alpha. He was living up to the role.

He'd keep our packs from killing one another, and in the meantime, I'd see what Shadow was up to.

Because if anyone knew where Katlyn was, it would be the leader of the Midnight Pack.

KATLYN

Pure exhaustion pushed me through a full night of sleep.

A beautifully dreamless night. No alphas. No magical potions.

Just sleep.

And it was Lyle's whistling that woke me up.

My heavy eyelids didn't want to open, especially when I felt entirely too warm and my stomach twisted.

Must be hungry, I decided.

And definitely too close to the fire.

When I opened my eyes, I frowned, because the hearth only held ash.

It had clearly burned out a while ago.

And while I was indeed hungry, my stomach twisted with familiar knives.

Ones that had more to do with my wolf than with nourishment.

My heat isn't over. Seriously?

Lyle had pounded me within an inch of my life. I was blissfully sore, but somehow, it hadn't resolved my issue.

If anything, it'd made it worse.

Yet, he sounded happy. I tried to pull myself together as I listened to him gather a pack.

"I know you're awake, little flower," he finally said after I'd been silent for at least fifteen minutes.

Clearing my throat, I slowly eased up. My vision wavered and I held a hand to my head and groaned.

A wave of incredible need washed over me, making me dizzy.

"Hey, everything all right?" Lyle knelt at my side and reached out to touch me, but I flinched away. He frowned, but closed his fingers into a fist.

"Fine," I said, then hissed against the pain. "Just... a headache."

A lie.

A big, fat, ugly lie.

He hummed. I wasn't sure if he actually bought it, but he was going to let it go.

And for that, I was grateful.

"Well, headache or not, there is still game out there than needs killing." He offered me my bow. "Care to join me? Maybe it'll get your mind off things."

I glanced up at him. His beautiful brown eyes held specks of green, just like they had lately, giving him an incredible allure that drew me in.

Desire flared in my core, but I shoved it down.

Hard.

He wanted to pretend like nothing had changed, apparently. So, I'd go along with it. "Hunting," I said, testing out the word. "Yeah. I can do that."

He gave me a soft smile, then placed my bow on the

ground between us. "Great. I'll take the lead. You can catch up."

He left before I could say anything, letting the door close on its own on his way out.

Cursing, I worked up the strength to get up.

There was the small matter of birth control to tend to, so I found the required herbs in Aunt Daliah's collection. She had everything on hand, including what I needed to make sure Lyle and I didn't have a child.

That was the last thing I needed. This dead world didn't need another innocent soul to devour.

That done, I snatched up the bow and placed it on the table. Then I put on my leathers and worked my hair up with a tie.

The practiced moves seemed to ground me. Hunting was something we often did together, but the intimate ache running through my center assured me that we weren't just hunting partners anymore.

Unless he regrets it, my unhelpful brain supplied.

My wolf decided to reply to that thought. *If he doesn't want you, then there are many alphas that do. We should go find them.*

Her cravings were going to be the death of me.

"So now you're speaking to me?" I asked her as I applied wax to the string of my bow. My aunt had supplies of all sorts, including wax. Although she hated when I used it, complaining that her stock came from beeswax which she'd suffered many stings to procure. I had some tallow wax in my old room, but my mother wasn't going to let me back in there.

A pang of guilt and grief hit me as that train of thought

threatened to run off on its own. I clamped it down and focused on the task at hand.

Yes. I think a hunt will do some good.

My wolf didn't reply to me as I left the hut. She seemed to struggle to stay sentient lately. Perhaps it had something to do with the heat, or the fact that I wasn't going to an alpha wolf to *take care* of things.

Unless Shadow summoned me again, that wasn't an option. And I wasn't even sure if I wanted it to be.

Right now, I was tired of this heat.

I was tired of being at the mercy of my basic impulses.

So I fell into old habits, looking for broken branches or grooves in the ground to see where Lyle had gone.

I couldn't find anything on first glance, so I ventured west. Animals had steered clear of the new creek, for some reason, but I knew there was a marshy area of the forest where many preferred to scavenge for food.

That was the best area for game, and that was likely where I would find my hunting partner.

My human instincts slowly took over as I slipped through the forest.

It was late morning, meaning the best hunting hours had passed, but I didn't mind a challenge. It felt good to work with the pattern of the forest winds, making sure my scent wouldn't be picked up by potential game while I also tracked Lyle.

A small victory made me smile when I found a missing patch of moss. He was excellent at keeping his footsteps quick and light, as well as avoiding any branches that might give him away—but he had a penchant for scraping moss.

The direction of the scrape suggested he'd turned north, which was odd. There wouldn't be game that way. The storms did a pretty good job of wiping out life and even if this area of the forest had seen some revival, heading towards wolf territory wasn't a good idea.

Not when I was being hunted.

"Why would you go this way?" I whispered to myself as I followed the new path.

I frowned when I spotted signs that Lyle had gotten careless.

Kneeling, I examined a broken twig that had been severed clean through the middle, indicating he'd been moving fast.

Worry started to creep over my heated skin when I spotted grooves from heavier footprints.

I followed them until I spotted Lyle staring over a clearing.

"Lyle, what is—"

My sentence cut short when I reached his side.

Because I saw what had his attention.

The storms were here.

KATLYN

"What in the name of the gods?" I breathed when I stared at the invisible wall as incredible winds beat against it.

"Your aunt put up a protection barrier, but it's not enough," Lyle said as his hand reached out for me.

Electricity crackled through my limbs when his fingers threaded through mine, but I couldn't bring myself to pull away.

I was too stunned by what I was seeing.

And confused.

Winds tore through the forest on the other side. Massive trees that had stood for hundreds of years collapsed and shook the ground.

But I couldn't hear a thing. It was as if we were contained in a bubble of silence while the world fell apart all around us.

Then a crack appeared, running straight through the barrier, revealing its silver tones.

Sound leaked through, allowing me to hear the angry

howls of the storm raging on the other side. Rain spattered through the growing opening and a frightening crack shrieked through the sky.

"The storms aren't supposed to be here," I said. The storms only came before a High Moon, not after it. We always had time to gather Moon Blossoms to put up protective barriers around our houses. The squalls had always been relatively predictable.

And while I knew the magic existed, I'd never seen a barrier like the one shielding an entire segment of the forest.

Except, it clearly wasn't holding.

"I know," he said, tugging me closer to his side. "Listen to me, Katlyn. We don't have much time. Your aunt explained to me that she put up barriers around the hut. They protect against the storms—but they also hide *you*."

I blinked at him a few times. "She's been able to make barriers like this the whole time I've been alive? Then why hasn't she safeguarded the village?"

His jaw flexed. "She *has* been. Why do you think the storms rarely make it this far? They're the worst during the High Moon and that's usually when there's a breach."

A crack thundered through the sky, sending the barrier ripping like silk over a blade.

The wolf inside of me snarled, awakening against the danger.

Run, silly human, she told me.

But it was the Goddess spirit inside of me that made me stand my ground.

She was familiar with these storms. She had created them, after all, but they weren't supposed to be like this.

Dark threads of vile sickness wove through the clouds and bled across the trees everywhere the rain touched. It seeped into the ground and shadows billowed like boils, infecting the soil with its illness.

"Corruption," I said, really *seeing* it for the first time. "Lyle, we have to stop this. It's destroying everything."

The Goddess inside of me was so weak, so drained.

And what frightened me most of all was if I concentrated, I could feel that sickness *inside* of me.

The ground lurched, making me yelp as my feet swept out from under me.

I lost Lyle's grip as I tumbled downward. Sharp pains speared my side as I rolled against stones and sharp branches.

My wolf reacted, supplying me with claws to try and gain purchase, but my momentum had me careening straight toward the breach in the protective barrier.

I screamed when the rain pummeled my face. A burning sensation that I had only felt once before seeped into my skin and sent my extremities on fire.

Run! my wolf shouted, and she didn't have to ask me twice.

I scrambled to my feet and clawed against wet muck as I climbed.

My breath came in sharp gasps and adrenaline overrode the pain.

It *burned*.

My leathers did little to protect me from the acidic rain. It allowed me to move unhindered, but left my arms and chest exposed.

My vision narrowed to a dark tunnel as I sank my claws into the muck, forcing myself upward another step.

I'm not going to make it.

I'm going to die here after everything.

I felt my alphas pierce my mind, their panicked emotions an unwelcome onslaught.

But it gave me insight enough to realize that Kane still hadn't recovered. Something horrible had happened to him and his soul was a fractured ember in the distance.

I'd shut myself off from him and now I wondered if that had been protective instinct.

Because something was wrong.

My other alphas seemed to lift me up, forcing my legs to work and my arms to climb.

Vern gave me his wisdom, showing me which rocks were stable and which were weak.

Dash gave me courage, overcoming my doubts with his confidence.

Ryker pushed me up through sheer faith, believing in me even when I didn't believe in myself.

And Shadow... he told me to pull myself together, because he wasn't done with me yet. The mark on my leg pleasantly burned with his promise.

It almost helped me reach the top of the broken patch of land the storms had decimated, but when I looked up, it was Lyle who was determined to get me the rest of the way.

"Take my hand, little flower," he said.

With the last of my strength, I launched myself upward, clasping his wrist with my grip.

His skin sizzled where the dark rain touched him, but he didn't let me go. Instead, he hauled me up into his arms.

And he lifted me, his forest-speckled eyes the last thing I saw before I succumbed to the dark.

KANE

"Kaitsja!" I screamed.

She was hurt.

She was dying.

Fuck!

Snarling, I thrashed and lurched against my chains, but as I had discovered in the past few days, they wouldn't break no matter how hard I tried.

Even against my rage.

Today was different, though. Something dark rolled outside the dungeon walls. Something *wrong*.

It was the very same entity that was attacking Kaitsja, and it would *pay*.

As if in retaliation for my threat, a crack broke through my dungeon walls, dousing the dim area with sudden light.

Not sunlight, but a bolt of energy from the storm.

Pain lanced through my extremities as it ripped through me. My wolf howled and my spirit roared.

Dark energy swirled throughout my chest, darkening

my senses as the chains binding my wrists and ankles crackled under the opposing power.

Fuck this magic. Fuck this confinement.

I. Was. *Done.*

With a roar, I yanked and finally—*miraculously*—my restraints gave way. Victory surged in my chest as I shattered the chains. What had once been impossible to break was now brittle and weak.

The impact sent shards of the metal ripping through skin and muscle, but I couldn't feel the bite.

Not when She was hurt.

Not when the storm raged outside, calling me to Her.

Blistering rain ran down my chest and soaked my tattered pants.

Screams and shouts from above indicated that my pack was working to establish a barrier. The storms had never attacked us like this—but our Goddess had never been hunted before, either.

Feel Her wrath, I growled, my sentiment an unspoken roar that rolled with the thunder terrorizing the landscape.

I'd been the alpha of my pack for years. I had guarded them and guided them, but now I wasn't so sure if they deserved my protection.

Not until Kaitsja was safe.

Not until She declared their fate for failing Her.

I marched through the broken dungeon beneath the mansion and clawed my way up to the surface. The storms hadn't attacked me.

They had *freed* me.

The cave where I kept prisoners was visible from my

vantage point. Although, the cave was empty if memory served. I couldn't remember why. Certainly there were plenty of souls deserving of punishment.

Like the alphas I had freed. Why had I released them? They'd been upgraded to the mansion's dungeon. It was a safer area and closer to the core of my pack's power.

They didn't realize the blessing I'd given them. It had likely made them stronger and closer to Kaitsja. Now, I regretted it, because they didn't deserve Her. No one did.

Not even me, but I would do everything I could to slay Her enemies and sacrifice their hearts in Her name.

I stared at the cavern that looked like a wide-open maw as I plotted all the ways I could make those who opposed Her suffer before they died. The area intrigued me and seemed to circulate the worst of the storms from its epicenter.

It was beautiful, like a tempest of destruction and death.

Fitting.

There should have been a wall to impede my view, but my compound was in shambles. Groups of wolves worked together, their hands in the air, sending Moon Magic to fuel protective barriers.

Silver walls rose like a massive bubble, working to encase the compound with impressive energy.

I had taught them well.

They don't know we're here, my wolf said, prowling in the back of my mind. *The Goddess deserves the blood of those who failed Her.*

Through the haze of red, I resisted the urge to shred into the unsuspecting wolves.

Julian was the first to notice my escape. He sacrificed any sense of self-preservation as he ran to me and held up a hand.

"Kane, listen to me. Your eyes still have a red ring, so whatever is going through your head right now *isn't you*."

Wasn't me? Perhaps it wasn't. But that was only because I'd held my wolf back when I should have let him free.

"You," I growled, circling my prey as I chose Julian to be the first to endure a slow death. "You restrained me and kept me from the Goddess. Now She hurts, and you are the one who is going to pay."

My second was one of the oldest members of my pack, as well as one of the most skilled in a fight.

Yet he used his words instead of his fists. That was one of his faults, and a reason he would never be alpha. "Kane," he snapped.

A snarl escaped my lips. "Alpha," I corrected him.

He growled in return. "I need you to pull yourself together, friend. You call yourself alpha, yet you threaten one of your own when we're under attack." He pointed at the rolling clouds. "That is your enemy right now, not me."

A crash of thunder ripped through the compound, the bolt sending splinters of wood and broken Moon Blossoms at our feet. The debris pelted my skin, leaving tiny wounds that quickly healed.

"Reinforcement on this side!" one of the wolves shouted, then a few of them realized I was there.

"Alpha! Thank the Goddess. We need your strength."

I scoffed, then lurched for Julian. He was fast, but

nowhere near fast enough for my reflexes. Darkness bled through my fingers from where I touched him, making him growl as if in pain.

Yet my body was the one scarred from magical restraint. I shoved my damaged arm in Julian's face, then showed my pack. "If you wish for my strength, why have you caged me? Why have you turned your backs on your alpha?"

Julian tried to reply, but I took him by the throat and lifted him off his feet.

He was a powerful wolf—one who could emerge as an alpha in his own right if he ever decided to challenge my authority.

The fact that he hadn't evolved was a testament to his weakness. I didn't need weak members in my pack.

Which made him expendable.

I began to squeeze…

"*Kane*," a feminine voice called.

I jolted at the delicious sound—Kaitsja!

She was here.

And She needed me!

Throwing Julian aside, I turned toward the source of Her call. It had been faint, but unmistakable.

The storms sent twisting winds to the ground, swirling and ripping up the soil everywhere it touched. The devastation should have terrified me—instead, it reinvigorated me. It called to the bloodlust and rage permeating my soul and made it flourish.

Made it *burn*.

I stepped into the tempest and held out my hands, exposing my skin to the acid rain.

"Kaitsja, I'm here."

Her voice rolled through the clouds, demonstrating Her powers as a Goddess. It sent chills up my spine and sent my heart pounding in my chest.

This way, Kane. Come to me, my mate.

Wolves shouted from behind me and I felt their magic attempting to wall off the rain.

I left them to their devices, finding them beneath me as I ventured into the storms.

My Goddess called me.

My Goddess *wanted* me.

I felt Her lust and Her desire radiating from the epicenter of the storms.

She was in the cave! Of course.

It was where I had first Claimed Her. It was where we had finalized our union, and it was where She now waited for me to return to Her.

Somehow, She was at the center of these storms. This destruction was Her wrath at those who had disappointed Her.

That's why the storms had freed me. That's why it made me feel so *alive*.

I followed the sound of Her call, the blissful tones of Her voice a drug to my senses.

The storms raged in a swirl of chaos and destruction, but it all ended when I stepped into the cave.

Silence engulfed me and I knew I was in the center of the storms.

"Kaitsja," I said. Her name echoed off the cavern walls.

"This way, Kane," She whispered in return.

The tunnel She called me from was dark, but I

ventured into it anyway. Shadows embraced me and called to a deeper part of me, one that craved secrets and torment.

Desire flared in my soul when I found Her.

My Goddess.

My Queen.

Shadows licked around Her silver form. All the Moon Blossoms were gone, but it was as if She'd devoured them all and now She was a beacon of magic.

The storms were a new power, one that I didn't fully understand, but I would certainly embrace.

It was a force to be feared and respected.

I fell to one knee and bowed my head. "Kaitsja, my Goddess."

She approached and grazed Her fingers under my chin, guiding me to look up into her perfect face.

Except, it was difficult to focus on her features.

She was just as I remembered Her, but at the same time… not.

"I need you, Kane," She said, Her words dripping with sensuality.

She slipped Her silver dress from her shoulders and the material pooled at her feet.

Her body was certainly as I remembered it. All smooth, supple skin and delicious curves.

I reached out to touch Her, but frowned when a ripple of darkness shimmered over her skin.

Something wasn't right.

What of the grief I sensed? The pain?

"Where have you been?" I asked as I pulled my fingers away and gazed up at Her.

Her fingers trailed down my cheek. Her disappointment was palpable, but She was being patient with me.

"I've been building the storms that saved you, my mate. I have grown tired. All of this energy... it has drained me." She pulled at my arm until I stood. She wrapped my hand around Her waist and pillowed Her breasts on my chest.

She should have been warm.

But She was cold like wet rain on a starless night.

"Give me your magic, Kane. Give me everything." When I didn't respond, her eyes widened in anger, flaring with magic. "Or did your vow have hollow promises? You promised that your life was mine to use as I saw fit. Right now I want you inside me, Alpha. I want you to help me *live*."

My nostrils flared as I pulled away.

Because this wasn't right. Kaitsja never called me alpha. It was a term She wasn't familiar with.

I sniffed the air. There was a floral scent, but it reminded me of nightshade.

Not jasmine.

"Who are you?" I snarled as I extended my claws.

"My mate, it's me," the female who looked like Kaitsja said as she batted her eyelashes. Her feigned innocence was as shallow as her words.

Snarling, I wrapped my fingers around her slender throat, backing her against the wall.

If this had been my mate, I would have been overcome with the need to claim Her right here, right now.

But *she* didn't smell like Kaitsja. And *she* wanted my magic, wanted my power.

Things that *my* Kaitsja never cared about. Her love was genuine, as were Her desires.

I would kill this imposter for daring to pretend to be the Goddess.

But first, I would learn her true identity.

"Who. Are. You?" I asked, punctuating each word with a growl.

She struggled for air, so I lessened the squeeze on her neck so she could answer me.

Except a response wasn't what she offered. Instead, she spoke foreign words that rushed around me with dark shadows.

Invisible needles punctured my skin and rammed into my temples, forcing me to release the female. I snarled as I fell to one knee.

Pain wasn't enough to subdue me, but this was agony unlike anything I'd ever felt. It rushed through my body and tore with a thousand tiny bites. Pressure built in my skull and I panted in response.

"I'm someone who is trying to help you," she replied.

Her voice had changed, but it still held a magical lilt to it that distorted the tones.

I blinked up at the mixture of silver and black wisps of power. The texture reminded me of silk as it swirled around her, obscuring her true face from view.

"You're... killing me," I said, pointing out that this was definitely the opposite of helping. The needles melted, leaving behind liquid fire through my veins. I groaned and braced myself against the pain.

My wolf snarled and tried to cool me with his magic, but it wasn't enough to keep the agony at bay.

She sighed as if exasperated. She threaded her fingers through my hair and if I hadn't been burning alive, I would have relieved her of the appendage. "My dear alpha. I'm afraid it's time that I save you from yourself. The moment you offered your life to the Moon Guardian, I knew you couldn't do this on your own."

I blinked through the waves of magic and agony as my eyes watered.

This was a wolf from my own pack.

Kill her, my beast growled.

My teeth ached to rip her throat from her body. My claws itched to plunge into her chest and admire her beating heart before it went silent.

Such treachery was the ultimate insult.

"The only thing I will be doing is wearing your entrails as a crown," I vowed, snarling up at the obscured wolf.

I didn't know where she had gotten such power. She seemed to be the source of the storms and the Corruption that the Hunters were so worried about.

And now I knew why they were concerned. Its darkness was infecting me, *consuming* me.

"I'm the Conduit," she said, using the term that described the medium Calamity used to spread chaos and death throughout the Hunters' realms. It had come here to continue its dark work. "But now, I share this gift with you. Embrace your destiny, Kane, Alpha of the Moon Pack. You are half of the Conduit of Calamity and I am your Queen."

A groan escaped me as an icy chill settled in my chest, blocking off my air and threatening to take me under.

I wrapped my fingers around her ankle, attempting to bring her down where I could bite and end this.

She easily stepped away from my claws, seemingly unaffected by the slashes I'd left behind.

She bled black, not red.

As she knelt, I endured the sinking reality that I was not going to win this battle. "Kaitsja is my Queen," I said. "Not you."

She could fill me with her dark power.

She could try to subdue me with foreign magic and weighted chaos, but I would not change my loyalties. I had vowed to protect Kaitsja and give her my life—that was something that could never be undone.

The female's dark eyes blinked as her face slowly bled with magic, revealing her features.

I stared when I recognized the white hair, the long, delicate face and almond eyes of one of my most trusted wolves.

Althea.

She ran her fingers down the side of my face. "She has a hold on you, my mate. When I help you kill her, you'll see who she truly is."

I snarled, but she shushed me and cupped my face with both of her hands. The cold pain had turned into a numb sensation, leaving me feeling heavy.

"Shh, my mate. The process is almost complete, and we have time to help you adjust. The Moon Guardian must complete her task of uniting the packs, as intended. She must be fully mated to all of them, and then when she dies, she'll take their souls with her, fully decimating the packs once and for all. However, your anchor will be

Calamity, will be *me*. And *then* you can take your mantle as the Wolf King. We will gather all of the fractured packs and unite them under *us*. Then they will know true strength, true *power*."

What in the moonlight was she going on about?

Had Calamity destroyed her mind?

Or had she been the one to invite it into our world in the first place?

Goddess. I was such a fool. Althea had been pulling the strings the entire time.

My desire to kill her was wavering. The cold magic wanted me to cooperate. It called Kaitsja the Champion of Calamity, one that needed to die for its mission to be accomplished.

It had tried one-on-one battles with the Champion before and that had failed.

Then it had learned with Dante's mate that infiltrating into the Champion's mate-circle was quite effective.

The Moon Goddess was a test—a means by which to infect the Champion and her mates.

I panted as the dark magic merged with my soul, forcing its knowledge and desires on me. I could sense what it wanted. There would be no pack left to reign. I would not become king.

There would only be death, chaos, and endless war. That's what Calamity ultimately wanted. It was a mindless force, one that the realms didn't fully understand or know how to control.

It would take a miracle to fend it off.

Or the power of a fully awakened Goddess. If Kaitsja

became Queen before Althea, perhaps She could free me of this darkness.

Or kill me.

I really didn't care, as long as She survived.

My body gave out as I slumped against Althea. She cocooned me against her chest and stroked my hair.

"Rest, my king. And when you wake, our trial will begin."

My eyes closed of their own accord, but my wolf prowled with the power of bloodlust still strong in his spirit.

Perhaps it was the only thing that had kept me lucid enough to mentally fight Althea and the full magic of Calamity at her fingertips. She had sold her soul to its power and was trying to take me down with her. One I would go along with, for now.

I would play her little game, because out of her rambling came some wonderful news.

Kaitsja was alive and well, and she was on the path to finish her mateship with the alphas of all the packs.

Meaning she would only grow in strength, and when it came time to face Calamity, I would rely on Her to free me of this cold prison.

And together, we would destroy Althea.

Soon, I promised my wolf.

Soon, there will be blood. Soon there will be pain.

Althea is our target, and her death will begin the Goddess's reign.

Go, beast. Pass on the message that it is time to coronate a new Queen.

SHADOW

"The storms are maintaining over Mystic territory," Freas said on the comm device as rain beat against the window. "They don't seem to be getting any larger after the initial growth, but they aren't weakening, either."

I chose to keep the phone pressed to my ear as I listened to the report. My room was supposed to be soundproof, as was the norm for shifters, but I didn't trust others to not somehow be listening in. Although, the storm raging outside would help drown out the sound.

"Casualties?" I asked.

"Yes, in the hundreds. And the counts are still coming in. Our pack has suffered the least, of course, at approximately sixty-four for those still trapped out in the open. Cause of death is mostly from landslides."

"And those who returned to the city, as ordered?" I asked. I didn't like my pack out in the open, and it seemed that my hunch had been correct in ordering the pack to refuge.

"Hmm. No deaths city-bound to be accounted for that I'm aware of."

I leaned back with a sigh. Normally, I didn't like to earn the respect of my pack through loss, but my order had likely saved numerous wolves. It would show that I was an alpha who had their backs.

I just hoped my pack saw it that way.

"If there are any still out there, find them and tell them to return here," I ordered.

Freas hummed his agreement. "Crescent City has strong buildings that protect against the winds. The worst of the storms are isolated over Mystic territory and have edged into Valiance and Soldier territory as well. The city will be the safest place for the time being."

My grip tightened on the phone. By Mystic Territory, I suspected that had something to do with Kane's pack.

But it was the last part of the sentence that made my heart skip a beat.

I leaned forward in my chair, staring into the fire burning in the room's small hearth as spattering continued on the window. "That means the storms have crossed the last human settlement."

It was presumably an unpopular view to keep the humans alive, but a storm like that could easily wipe them out, making the race extinct in our realm.

Freas hesitated, and I could almost picture him scratching his chin that likely had thick stubble on it by now. I doubted that he'd paused to consider that potential issue. "Yes, I suppose so."

"Julian's account suggested that Kaitsja was with the humans," I said, more to myself than Freas. None of my scouts had found her, which meant either the humans were better at hiding than we thought, or she was receiving magical assistance.

Either way, if she was near the human settlement, that would put her in the direct path of the storms.

That explained the surge of panic I'd felt from her earlier in the day. We weren't fully mated, but my bite had established a certain level of courtship that tied our souls.

Marking one's intended mate was how a mate-bond was initiated. While it required sex to finalize and make the bond permanent, I'd already dedicated my soul to hers.

And now I wished that I had pushed her to finalize the bond, because I couldn't sense her current state. She was alive, but that was all the information I was going to get.

It seems I'm going to be using another Moon Nectar vial tonight.

Of course, I had intended to use one anyway. Very little could keep me away from the heaven that was between her legs.

The image of her captivating face formed in my mind. Her fuckable lips open on a heavy pant while I used my tongue and my fingers to—

An urgent knock at the door jolted me from my thoughts.

"Stay at the Outpost and find out what's going on with these storms. Report back to me tomorrow on what you find," I told Freas, then clicked off the phone and set down my glass of whisky.

It was my preferred drink, even if it was a drink that had evolved from humans. Some spiked it with Moon

Dust. That was an ointment used for healing, but also had euphoric properties for a wolf shifter to give the drink more of its intended kick.

I opened the door to find Dash and Ryker waiting for me. Ryker leaned against the doorframe, a strong streak of silver in his hair hanging over his eyes. He was dripping with dark droplets, suggesting they'd just braved the tempest raging outside. Although, it didn't seem to bother him.

He leaned in and took a quick scan of the room. "Hmm, yes. I see why you couldn't make the meeting. Working out hierarchy and all that. You must be showing you're alpha by how much you can sleep. Truly suffering here, Shadow."

Dash crossed his arms, sending his already massive biceps bulging. "I see whisky."

I waved them inside. "Help yourself."

Dash ventured in first, heading straight for my drink. Before I could tell him where the glasses were, he grabbed mine and drained it.

I glowered at him.

Ryker prowled around the room, seemingly uninterested in the human beverage.

"I was going to punch you in the face. I've since changed my mind," he informed me matter-of-factly.

I raised a brow. "I didn't spike the whisky with Moon Dust, if that offends you."

That was how many wolves enhanced the otherwise bland drink.

Although, I had been ingesting Moon Nectar and using it to summon the Goddess he so revered to make her come on my tongue. *That* might be cause for slight irritation for Ryker, so I chose not to bring that up.

He cracked his knuckles. "We have less than a month before the Hunters end the truce. They want us to hand over Katlyn so they can cleanse her, or some shit." He blew his hair out of his eyes. "You're the only one who knows Logan, so if you had been at the meeting, perhaps we could have negotiated more time."

My shoulders relaxed at the news. "A whole month?" I poured myself a new drink and took a spot by the fire. "That's amazing. I honestly expected only a few days from Dante."

The rain beat harder against the windows and I waited for Ryker to say something, but he only glared at me.

Dash held out his glass. "Another."

I poured, then indicated a cabinet to the drenched alphas. "Towels are over there. You both are leaving black stains on the carpet."

While this wasn't my territory, it was a room I had grown attached to over the years. I did not intend to be stuck with stains.

Ryker frowned, then looked at his hands. "What are you talking about?"

Dash extended one of his legs, growing entirely too comfortable in my favorite chair. "It's just a little water, Shad. Relax."

I frowned. "You're telling me you can't see that?" I pointed at the dark spots around Ryker's boots and then the drizzle of black down Dash's fingers. "You were out in the storms and the water on you is black."

Both alphas shared a look.

"Well, that can't be good," Dash said as he placed down his glass and went to the indicated cabinet. He grabbed a towel, and then tossed another to Ryker. "It took us an entire day to get back into the city after the storms hit. Might not even made it if Ryker hadn't shown me high ground less prone to landslides. We've been out there for a while." He frowned at the window. The lashing winds seemed to have only gotten worse as the pane rattled in its frame. "Since when do they come this far, anyway?"

I had my suspicions, but the moon was almost in position and I was itching to summon Katlyn. I needed to know that she was all right.

And I needed to continue our courtship.

Something that would be difficult to accomplish with two other alphas in the room.

Or, perhaps it was the perfect opportunity to demonstrate my dedication to her.

Alphas were possessive, arrogant creatures. However I wanted to prove to Katlyn that I wasn't like the wolves she knew.

If my hunches were correct, none of us were.

"Would you prefer to speculate about the storms, or would you indulge me with a little chat with our mate?"

Both alphas stared at me with confusion, so I dug out the vial from the inside of my suit pocket. I preferred to go shirtless, but there was something about being in the city when it came to modern fashion.

Plus, I hoped that Katlyn would like it. She had told me she wanted the man, not the wolf. I fully intended to show her I was just as much of a man as I was anything else.

Although when it would come time to claim her, I would be all *beast*.

Soon, I told my prowling wolf. *Soon you'll have your taste.*

Ryker's eyes darkened as his gaze landed on the sacred vial. "Why am I not surprised you've found new ways to blaspheme our Goddess?"

Dash ran his finger over the edge of his glass, sending a musical tone ringing through the room. "Let me guess. That's why you've been holed up here while we've all been stuck negotiating with the Hunters, hmm? Does that give you a mental link to talk to Katlyn?"

I grinned, unable to resist showing my sharp teeth. "Oh, it does so much more than that. It summons her spirit here and gives her corporeal form as long as the moon lasts." I glanced at the window. "Although, the last time I used it, I had full access to the sky. I'm not sure how well it'll work now."

Ryker's nostrils flared. "She was here, alone, with *you*?"

I couldn't help the tick of my jaw. "Yes."

Dash gave me a level stare. "What happened?"

The recollection of my night with Katlyn ran through my mind. While we had talked and bonded, the most prominent memories were her coming on my tongue.

But it was more than lust. She was special and I would dedicate my life to helping her achieve her destiny. Our time together only enforced my desire to help her.

Katlyn's fate had become clear to me. She would unite the wolves. She would repair the devolution of shifter kind that was responsible for darkness and death, such as I had experienced in my own pack.

A part of me wanted to brag to Dash and Ryker just to get a rise out of them. But my goal right now was to show Katlyn how much of a man I could be—to earn her acceptance so that I might help her and be of use to her goals.

My beast wished to keep her all to himself, but a true man puts his mate's needs and desires above his own.

And to do that, I would have to *share*.

"I helped her with her heat," I said honestly, not to brag, but to entice them. "Or tried to, anyway. I only seemed to manage to make her come a few times."

Dash went still and Ryker... *disappeared*.

Ryker's face appeared before mine a moment later and I resisted the urge to flinch. He had the worst scar out of all of us from ascension to pack alpha, and he was perhaps the most good-looking if I were being honest. A jagged line ran down his otherwise divine-blessed face.

I stared at him, unmoving, as I marveled at the darkness swirling in his eyes.

The storms had definitely done something to him. Wolves were familiar with the storms and their acidic impact. It often killed plants and wildlife, but it didn't do much to wolves as far as I was concerned.

Yet, we'd never been exposed to storms of this magnitude and length of time.

Ryker was changing.

I had never been snuck up on. I was a Midnight Pack wolf. Stealth, speed, and subterfuge was my strength. Ryker was a Mystic. He was likely the type to have his muzzle stuck in an old book, or working out some prophecy or other from one of those loony wolves in his pack that were permitted to eat Moon Blossoms. It was

such a deprived source to his pack that it gave them hallu-
cinations—or that was the rumor, anyway. After getting
to know Ryker, I found that he was devoted, but not
crazy.

Yet now he had a distinctly psychotic expression as he
licked his lengthened fang. His wolf had abandoned him,
but the idea of tasting his mate seemed to have finally
enticed him to return. "Is she still in heat?"

I nodded. "Yes, I suspect so. It's why I was planning to
summon her tonight."

Ryker's nostrils flared again. "Without us?" He tsked.
"We are *all* her mates, Shadow."

It was a statement. A challenge, one I had no intention
of fighting.

"We are," I confirmed as I held out the vial. "Perhaps
you'll have better luck with her than me, but we all will
follow her lead, understood?"

"Of course," he said with a low rumble to his words.
He eyed the vial with hunger. "She is my Goddess,
Midnight Alpha. I trust her in my presence much more
than yours."

Even if I had been a gentleman, he had a point. I'd
pushed her hard enough to make her come on my tongue.

Multiple times.

All while I knew that wouldn't help her with her heat,
not in the long run. She needed a wolf's appreciation for
sex, not a man's. She needed a knot, but she wasn't ready
for that. And my mark on her had likely only made things
worse.

Maybe Ryker would be more effective. Jealousy
squeezed my cock, but arousal made it pulse at the

thought of knot in her sweet pussy. Even if it wasn't my own.

I rested the vial in his waiting palm. "If you drink it all, I'll put a new scar on that pretty face of yours."

If he was faster than me, I didn't want to test what other attributes he'd earned from his exposure to the storms.

Perhaps Katlyn would have an outside perspective she could offer. The humans had to deal with the storms a lot more often than the wolves.

Not to mention she was the Moon Guardian.

Ryker dutifully uncorked the vial with his teeth, then took a light swig. His eyes fluttered closed as he swallowed. With a shiver, he handed the vial back to me.

I gave Dash a taste, then I finished it off.

Then we waited, and I was sure I wasn't the only one who prayed for our Goddess to hear our call.

Come to us and bless us, little wolf.

Your alphas want a word with you... and perhaps a little game.

One that involves showing you how much of a man I am, because a man puts his mate's needs above his own.

And right now, you need me to share.

All I ask is that I get to watch...

VERN

"Dig!" I shouted, ignoring the urge to shift into wolf form and tear into whoever was responsible for this level of carnage.

Except a wolf couldn't take on the storms. The wild tempest had hidden the source of our strength, the moon, and caused nature to turn against us.

We didn't stand a chance. Neither did the Hunters. Resulting in the odd sight of Hunters and wolves working together to dig up lost souls trapped in the latest landslide.

The border between Mystic and Valiance territory was the perfect combination of mud and mountains to encourage the type of shift in the soil that had already claimed hundreds of lives.

Xenos, one of the higher-ranking Hunters, stood at my side as we directed the rescue attempt from higher ground.

He leaned onto one knee. "That side is weak, you should send your mutts out."

I ignored the insult, as well as the unwarranted advice.

This was my territory. I knew the land better than anyone—especially a cocky-ass outsider with a penchant for killing.

"You worry about your *men*, and I'll worry about mine," I retorted. He wanted to name-call, but I wouldn't stoop to his level.

When the one-month truce was up, he'd receive my response by means of my teeth in his neck.

As if he guessed my thoughts, he gave me a wry grin. "It's killing you not to be able to use those teeth of yours, hmm? Just give it a try, beast. I never liked the idea of a truce. Dante doesn't have his head on straight to have agreed to it in the first place." He thumbed his blade. "We could end it early. Right here, right now."

While the Hunter was busy trying to goad me, one of his men was digging into a weak part of the cliff—a place my wolves knew to avoid.

"Order your men off," I snapped at him. The idiot was going to get more killed.

He laughed as he slowly drew out his blade, and then pointed it at me. "Trying to fool me, are you? I'm not falling for your wolfish tricks. I know for a fact we have some Hunters caught up in this landslide and they need to be rescued tonight. A Hunter can handle a lot more than you think. They'll be found alive, and I intend to *keep* them alive."

My senses picked up the subtle shift of soil and land. I suspected that the Hunter had just as good hearing as I did, but what he didn't have was a connection to this territory.

Being alpha wasn't just a title. I was a link to both my pack and the land, and right now, the ground was *shifting*.

"Move!" I shouted, my words echoing with the force of my growl.

What few wolves were near the area evacuated, but the Hunters looked up at us, then to Xenos as if waiting for his direction.

He only laughed.

Idiot.

I jumped from the cliff and shifted in the air. My bones snapped and fur sprouted across my limbs.

Shifting on demand was a new skill, one that likely had something to do with becoming the Moon Goddess's mate.

Once in wolf form, my senses picked up the stench of wet darkness behind a veil of trees.

Another wave of the rains were coming—and this was a big one.

Perhaps even bigger than the ones that had caused the latest landslides.

We had to get out of here. This rescue party was about to become a large group of victims if we stayed.

Hunters yelled as Xenos cried out nonsense that I was a wild beast out for blood. They didn't have time to react. The weak area of land shifted, sending the entire group sliding into the mud.

I acted fast, grabbing the nearest Hunter by the arm and dragging him screaming from a slow death.

He misunderstood my intentions and sharp pain burst in my side.

The ungrateful bastard had used a knife on me.

I dropped him before he could stab me again, but we'd already moved to a safer part of the slope. Land continued to give way just ahead of us, instantly covering up the remaining Hunters who hadn't reacted fast enough.

I glowered at the one I had saved. His orange eyes glowed with conflict, because he seemed to realize I'd been trying to help him.

Katlyn was still out there. I needed these idiots to help us find her—and then they could die. I'd gratefully help them along death's path once their usefulness ran out.

Shouts drew my attention as the wind picked up, sending tree branches cascading to the forest floor. The howl of the powerful gusts sounded like a beast.

It sounded like a wolf.

A strange tug on my spirit drew me toward the storms when I should have had the sense to run away.

What is this bizarre magic?

Something powerful was approaching, but it felt familiar. Strength was a virtue to be respected and revered.

Logic told me to turn away, but my beast stepped forward.

I'd learned by now to listen to him. He'd tried to tell me that Katlyn was our destined mate, that she had absorbed the Goddess, not killed our deity.

And now, my wolf urged me toward the storm, seemingly drawn to an entity that called to us with desperation.

Another howl rang out, this one more powerful and much closer.

My wolf threw our head back and released an echoing call, one that swept through the forest with ease.

The storms increased in strength and massive trees crashed all around me. The ground thundered and rumbled, but I didn't move.

A path carved around me as trees fell to the sides, giving me full view of an ethereal white wolf in the center of the tempest.

He was larger than any wolf I'd ever seen. Rain made up his fur and crescents of the moon were his eyes.

Darkness swirled all around him like a creature attempting to devour him whole. It formed an open-ended tunnel that threatened to close its giant maw.

I walked into it without hesitation, knowing that this white beast was Kane.

Or at least Kane's wolf.

Confirmation in the form of his greeting growl sent a ripple down my spine. My hackles rose, but not out of fear, but rather respect for the power of this beast.

Vern. You heard my call.

I'd never heard another wolf's voice in my mind, and neither had my beast. We cocked our head to the side and contemplated the conundrum.

My wolf wasn't sure how to reply, because we didn't seem able to replicate the mental link that Kane's beast had with us. Rain needled my skin as I shifted back into human form. My hair lashed around my eyes while I slowly stood, enduring the raging tempest that swirled through the dark tunnel.

I approached Kane's beast who was the source of light, as if he held a piece of the Goddess's Moon inside of himself. He glowed with powerful silver rays and was soft to the touch. My fingers slipped through the layers of his fur as I indulged in the need to connect.

"Tell me what's happened, Moon Alpha," I said, using the formal title rather than the term I'd been fonder of for Kane.

This was no Outcast. This was power incarnate, and just as I had grown to learn and accept Katlyn, so would I do with the Moon Pack's leader.

It was time to put aside old grievances and work together.

The wolf's crescent moon eyes glittered with magic as he watched me. He shook himself, sending rain splattering before he spoke inside my head again.

My human half has been infected by Calamity. Althea was the one that the Hunters call a Conduit, and now she is sending it into me.

My eyes rounded. That certainly didn't sound good.

Not just because I was growing to respect Kane, but because Kane was the only one of us fully mated to Katlyn. He had a connection to her on a spiritual level and I wasn't sure what would happen to our Goddess if she was bonded to a Corrupted mate.

"Tell me where you are," I said as I clenched the beast's fur in my fist. I met his muzzle with my nose, enraged that Katlyn was now at risk.

It surprised me that my anger was also because Kane was in danger, too.

Katlyn had bonded to him, and that made Kane a part of *me.*

The wolf shook his head. *Do not come for me. You must send the wolves to the city.*

I pondered that. "Why?"

The wolf's maw opened on a pant, resembling something like a smile. *Because it's time for a coronation. It's time for the wolves to bow to a Queen.*

Two days later...

I wasn't sure how Lyle had managed to carry my unconscious body all the way back to Aunt Daliah's hut in the full force of the storms.

But I was grateful.

My skin burned with the acidic remnants of the rain. The storms had never felt like this, and I'd been caught out in them before.

Last time, it had felt like power.

Now, it felt like an illness threatening to take me under.

I twisted and turned with the force of a raging fever as Lyle tended to me. He pressed a cup to my lips, urging me to take a sip, but it only made me cough.

My entire body succumbed to an endless tremor as I shook from the mixture of powerful of pain and dark magic.

"I'm here, my flower," he said, using soft tones and

tender caresses. "Would you like to try some bone broth again?"

I managed to shake my head, because my stomach lurched at the thought of putting anything inside of it.

I didn't need broth.

I needed an alpha's knot.

I needed wolf magic and the *moon*.

"You haven't eaten in days," Lyle said as he slowly smoothed damp strands stuck to my forehead. "You're going to have to try."

I couldn't answer him. I felt too weak, too desperate for something he couldn't give me.

My body reacted to Lyle. Every time he touched me, it seemed to sustain me enough to keep me alive, but it wouldn't eliminate the raging fever slowly taking me under.

A part of me wondered how long we could last like this. If we were somehow the only two people in our world and the storms were trying to take us with its final breath.

The winds rattled the windows and continued to rage outside. The powerful gusts lashed at our small refuge, making the entire thing creak and groan.

Whatever barriers my aunt had put up only seemed capable of keeping the hut in one piece.

As wood began to crack, I doubted even that might hold.

Despite the sense of impending doom, my wolf and the Goddess spirit inside of me had their eyes on a horizon I couldn't see. They'd been like this for two days.

At first I'd been confused, but now I wondered what they were looking for.

While my heat and some strange infection threatened to consume my body, the forces inside of me had their attention elsewhere.

I couldn't make sense of it until my body succumbed to unconsciousness once more and I felt the rise of the moon.

Yes, there, I whispered inside my mind.

I hadn't felt the power of the moon for two days and I reached out for it with a sense of desperation.

Its silver power rushed over me like a refreshing wave of cool water. A sigh escaped me as I slipped into a dreamlike state of peace.

This was a place away from the incessant pain and the rampaging fever.

Yet my wolf tugged me forward with a sense of expectation.

This way, she said inside my mind. *They're calling us.*

When the moon reached its apex, the Goddess spirit inside of me threaded her fingers around mine and launched me through the cosmos.

The moon glittered and revitalized us, sending us on a journey through the stars until we landed in a familiar suite where I had been courted by Shadow.

Except this time, he wasn't alone.

I curled my fingers in the bedsheets as I perched on the edge of the massive mattress. My slight weight sank into the plush bedding and my long hair draped over my naked breasts.

I'd been summoned before with clothes.

This time, I was naked.

And I recognized familiar alphas kneeling before me.

Both Dash and Ryker had their heads bowed in reverence while Shadow sat behind them in a chair.

He was fully clothed in a strange outfit—but it was attractive on him.

"It's called a suit and tie," he said, seemingly responding to my expression. He unbuttoned the vest and then lounged in his chair. A glass of golden liquid with ice was at his side and he toyed with it. A swallow stuck in my throat because even that motion was sensual.

I looked down, working to collect myself.

My body was still constructing, as if the power of the moon had some difficulty permeating the storms. My fingers were translucent, but growing more corporeal the longer I remained.

"We were worried you wouldn't come," Shadow continued, forcing me to meet his dark gaze again. "But it seems we just needed all of us here to have enough power to summon you."

That's when I noticed a figure in the doorway. He didn't come into the light where I could see him, but my wolf recognized him.

My nostrils flared as I took in the decadent scents in the room.

Cedar and thyme for Shadow.

Lemongrass and honey for Ryker.

Sandalwood and spice for Dash.

Vern… Ginger and sage made up his aroma.

I'd never taken such strong notice of their scents

before, but now I drew them in as if this was the oxygen my body had been lacking.

Kane was the only alpha missing from the concoction that had my thighs squeezing together. I missed his intoxicating mixture of pine and embers.

Although, my human form was still in Aunt Daliah's hut and Lyle's scents of firewood and earth were similar to Kane's.

In some ways, Lyle reminded me of the Moon Alpha, just in human form.

The eyes on me brought me back to the tension in the room.

None of them spoke.

Shadow continued to watch me as he ran his fingers over the edge of his glass. A look of desire and expectation swirled in his dark gray eyes.

As did a wry smugness that warned me he was planning something.

Ryker and Dash remained with their heads bowed. Their bodies were still. They wore pants, but no shirt, opting for the type of coverage I was more accustomed to when it came to the wolves.

Like Shadow, Vern watched me, too. His emerald gaze cut through the darkness with a different sort of expectation, one of nervousness and hesitation.

I wondered if Shadow had explained to them my newfound desire to give them a chance.

To accept them, even, if I was properly courted.

Because I'd made a promise to Luna. My sister never asked anything of me, but this was a vow I intended to keep.

She wanted me to "unite them." That could take on different forms, but my wolf seemed to think that meant accepting the alphas of all five packs.

Something I wasn't sure I was willing to do, but I was no longer opposed to the idea.

Glancing back at Shadow, I narrowed my eyes. I had voiced to him my desire for the *man*, not the wolf.

Perhaps that explained his strange outfit.

But it didn't explain the look on his face.

I raised my fingers, still finding them translucent, and I reached for the bedsheets to try and cover myself.

They cushioned beneath my touch, but with enough force I pushed straight through them as if I was a ghost.

Concerned, I decided to see what else I could touch. I stood, blushing hotly at my naked state.

Shadow didn't advert his gaze. Instead he raked it over me with a look that suggested he wanted to devour me.

Given that's exactly what he had done the last time I'd been summoned like this, I wondered if that was his intention.

Desire flared in the pit of my stomach and made me clench my thighs together.

If I wasn't corporeal, how would he touch me?

And even if he could, was his smugness because he expected us to have an audience?

I took in the rest of my alphas, wondering if he intended to make them watch.

I'd joined Kane before them all as a form of punishment, but somehow this felt like a punishment designed for me.

Because I was with Lyle? Did they even know about him?

Guilt tugged at my chest and I hated the conflict in my heart. Lyle was clearly jealous of my alphas. I doubted that they would accept him any more than my human counterpart did.

Not to mention that Lyle had fucked me within an inch of my life before any of these alphas had a chance to introduce me to their knots.

Another wave of desire thrummed through me at the idea of being *knotted*. That full feeling of bliss that Kane had provided was what my wolf truly craved.

And now I was in a room with four alphas, two of them kneeling for me.

I staggered and I reached out to Ryker on instinct. My fingers brushed through his hair and the contact snapped magic through my body.

Completing its transition into a fully corporeal state.

Ryker didn't move as I brushed his hair, and then I knelt before him to look into his face.

He didn't move until I placed a finger under his chin and tipped his face up to look at mine.

The lust in his gaze hit me straight in my belly.

Knives spun through my core in response, making me cry out and grip an arm over my middle.

Ryker held me by the elbow, keeping me from falling while Dash supported me from the other side.

"Your heat has gone on for too long, little Goddess," Ryker said with a strained tone.

His arousal was evident, making his pants tight around his hips as he remained inches from me.

Ryker was incredibly beautiful. I'd never noticed the smoothness of his features and the divine quality that made me want to lick him.

A jagged scar seemed out of place as it ran over his brow, past his silver eye, and over the arch of his cheekbone.

I traced it with a finger, wanting to heal the gash.

"Too long," I agreed, my voice thick with desire.

I wanted to be courted, but it seemed my wolf was growing impatient.

"But surely that's not why you all are here," I said, glancing back at Dash who branded my hips with his strong hands. Then I glanced at the silhouette that was Vern, and finally Shadow still remaining in his chair.

Although his pants had a noticeable bulge now that suggested he was definitely here to help me with my heat.

"Yes and no," he admitted. He glanced at the doorway. "Why don't you tell her what you told us, Vern?"

I followed his gaze to the darkness and waited for Vern to emerge, but instead he merely spoke. "Kane is being held by Althea. She claims to be the Conduit of Calamity that the Hunters warned us about—the entity that infected the Goddess within you. It's reaching all of us and slowly Corrupting us. Calamity seems to be the source of the storms—but it's only getting worse. Kane believes you're the only one who can stop her... by uniting the packs."

I blinked a few times as I tried to take all that in. Ryker and Dash held me steady, of which I was grateful.

There was a pained quality to Vern's voice that concerned me more than all the things he had just said.

"Come to me, Vern," I said.

Tension strung between us when he didn't obey.

Shadow was the first to correct him. "Our Goddess gave you an order, Alpha of the Valiance Pack."

A shift in the darkness indicated that Vern had heard him, then he finally left his refuge.

I drew in a gasp of air, shocked at the dark streaks bleeding through his veins. It gathered at his eyes, but didn't yet invade the perfect emeralds of his irises.

He frowned at my expression. "I'm not worthy to be in your presence, Katlyn. I tried to explain it to Shadow, but he insisted I drink the Moon Nectar."

"And it summoned her, just like I said it would," Shadow retorted. "Because she's our *fated mate*."

I knew that's what I was to them, but to hear Shadow say it out loud awakened fresh desire inside of me.

My heat returned as it burned down my extremities, nearly severing my connection to my body in the small hut with Lyle.

A tiny, almost indecipherable link remained, but I knew it was just enough to keep me alive.

Because right now, the full effect of denying my wolf's heat was upon me and I screamed as its raw force ripped through my core.

Ryker was the first to kiss me. He swallowed my scream as he cupped my face.

"I'm here, if you need me," he vowed.

Dash skimmed his teeth over my shoulder, promising the same with his touch alone.

Vern had ventured closer, but still remained out of reach. Concern pinched his eyebrows as his mouth parted, revealing sharp teeth as if he had partially shifted.

"Her scent…" he said as his nostrils flared.

Ryker licked my lower lip. "She's a true Omega in heat," he breathed with such reverence that I could only part my mouth in response and accept his attention.

"It hurts…" I complained, but Shadow was the one who shushed me.

He had somehow moved from his chair and now was at my side, between Ryker and Dash.

With his fingers pressed firmly on my clit.

"Then they will help you," he said, as if he wasn't the one making me see stars behind my eyes as he swirled his touch around in circles.

My hips moved with him, desperate for more.

"I can't," I said, knowing that this wasn't right.

Even if I wanted to accept them, I had to get to know them. I had to see the man behind the beast.

Shadow was the only one I had grown to learn and it was his touch I accepted as I moved my hips.

If I would take anyone's knot, then surely it must be his.

He nipped my ear in reprimand. "You wanted a courtship, little wolf. You wanted a *man*, and you know what a man does?"

I whimpered when he stopped his torturous little circles. He pulled away, then replaced the pressure with Ryker's fingers.

My wolf approved with a purr.

"A man gives his woman what she needs. And right now, you need the purest of us. You're a Goddess and you deserve to be worshipped." He backed behind Ryker, then guided Ryker's fingers in the same circular motions as if instructing him. "There isn't one among us more devoted than the Alpha of the Mystics, little wolf."

I panted when Shadow guided Ryker's fingers inside of me in a gentle thrust, making me feel both of them with the motion.

My back met Dash's hard chest as he rumbled his approval.

His hands remained on my hips, keeping me in place as he stood.

Ryker and Shadow followed us, their fingers both still inside of me, until Dash maneuvered us back to the bed. He sat with his legs on either side of me and his arousal pressing against my back.

He spread me, making me whimper with the vulnerability as I perched on the edge.

But I didn't stop them. My wolf wouldn't allow it.

And with a surge of cool Moon Magic over my skin, I realized the Goddess was in approval of this decision, too.

Ryker's gaze remained on mine, his pupils blown with desire, as he worked his fingers inside of me.

Shadow continued to instruct him while Vern watched.

"He's a virgin," Vern supplied, making my eyes widen. "He refused to touch any female until he found the mate his Goddess chose for him."

Ryker closed the small distance between us, his lips just above mine as he spoke. "I never expected to be mated to the Goddess herself," he said, the words stroking me like praise as he continued to pleasure me from below. "I hope you'll accept my prayer for forgiveness." Shadow slowly removed his fingers, leaving only Ryker touching me, then licked his fingers clean before he returned to his chair.

Now I understood why the Goddess approved of Ryker.

"Then you will knot me," I said with a voice that wasn't quite my own. I broke Ryker's gaze to look at Vern. "And all of you will bite me when it is done."

Because the Goddess inside of me knew that I didn't have to be knotted by all of the alphas to unite the packs.

I only needed their mark. My link to Shadow was firmly in place, proving it was possible.

They could earn my full acceptance into my mind and my body, but Ryker had already paid that price.

For that, he would be rewarded.

I turned my attention back to the Mystic Alpha. "Take off your clothes, Ryker. And *fuck me*."

RYKER

My Goddess had just told me to fuck her.

And I'd never been so terrified in all my life.

The human inside of her was experienced. I knew she was no virgin. The Goddess was another matter.

And it was the Goddess who had decided on me. The human was only following her lead. I could see the duality in her eyes as she accepted my touch.

Her skin turned silver.

Magic hummed through the air and seemed to wrap around my cock with a demand of its own.

Perhaps the Goddess had never mated in corporeal form, but she was sex incarnate.

She was pleasure itself.

I'd always been a devout follower of the Goddess, but something primal in me knew it was important *not* to obey.

Not when it came to her pleasure.

A Goddess wished for a show of strength, dominance

My fingers were already inside her sweet pussy and I stroked her just like Shadow had instructed me. Her body reacted with each movement, sending a gush of slick over my fingers and preparing her for all of the things I was going to do to her.

Just because I was a virgin didn't mean I wouldn't take my time.

If anything, I was more experienced in restraint than any of the others.

"You're going to come on my hand first," I told Katlyn, earning a fiery growl from her in response. I was glad I hadn't taken off my pants, because I required the barrier between us to see my intentions through.

I cupped my fingers and pressed on that spot inside of her a little more firmly.

Wetness coated my palm, telling me I had done something right.

She squirmed as if trying to dislodge me, but I would not make this a quick or unmemorable mating.

This was our first union, and I was going to make it fucking count.

"Hold her," I instructed Dash.

We hadn't been sure if Katlyn would want any of our knots, even though her heat was closing in on potentially fatal effects.

An Omega in heat required a knot or she would die. That was how our kind worked. Procreation was more difficult with our kind and not every female was capable of producing pups. When an Omega was born, instinct made it impossible to ignore the very real need to procreate.

I wasn't even sure if Katlyn understood what her heat meant. In normal circumstances, she was going to be pregnant by the end of the night.

But she'd already proven not to be the norm. Kane's introduction hadn't been during a true heat. She'd been needy, yes, but not like this.

Now, she was primed.

Except, we'd summoned her spiritual form, meaning this wouldn't impregnate her. That made this introduction much safer.

She would be introduced to the idea of a pup when she was ready.

And I hoped she would grace me with the opportunity to be the first father, but I would earn that role.

Right now, I was pleased to have earned her choice as the first to knot her after Kane.

Kane had earned the primary role, having never rejected her in the first place. I no longer begrudged him of that because I was still angry at myself for not seeing Katlyn for who and what she was.

My Goddess.

My destined mate.

As an apology, I squeezed her breast as I pleasured her. Dash kept her in place just as I had asked and that only seemed to arouse her more.

Her mouth opened on a pant as she took each thrust of my fingers, working her hips as much as Dash's grip would allow her to ride me.

"I need your cock," she demanded on a growl.

I would give her what she wanted, but not yet.

"You're going to have to earn that," I said, enjoying the snarl she released.

Dash pushed my hand out of the way and stroked her clit with his. "Silence that rebellious little mouth of hers," he said.

The sparkle in her gaze said she enjoyed that idea, so I did, letting her taste herself before I wrapped my hand around her throat and kissed her.

I didn't press hard; just let her know my power was here for her pleasure. For her delight.

She didn't take my kiss with submission. Instead, she fought my tongue with hers, seeming to demand more with every stroke until she bit my lip, drawing blood.

I hummed into her mouth, liking the violence of our mate. "Needy little Goddess," I said, then lowered my teeth to her breast.

She went still as I stroked her on the inside. Perhaps she expected me to bite, to mark, but I wouldn't. Not until I was satisfied she'd come enough times.

Not until I was inside of her and stretching her on my knot.

Instinct told me what to do as I circled my tongue around her peak. Then I drew it into my mouth and sucked.

She whimpered as her back arched.

That was a mistake, because it gave me better access to her.

I shoved another finger inside, preparing her.

Because I had a large cock and I knew it. It was one of the things my pack was known for, but I wouldn't reveal that to her quite yet.

Nor would I reveal the other little surprise my cock had in store for her.

Not until I'd fully worshipped her, first.

"Take your hand away," I instructed Dash.

He complied and returned his free hand to her neglected breast. She seemed to enjoy how he toyed with her nipple as I kissed lower.

I had wanted her to come on my hand, but I couldn't resist a taste.

My teeth skimmed her flat belly, then over her mound before I reached my destination.

Shadow's mark was still on her thigh. He'd warned us about it so we wouldn't be surprised, but I didn't receive the surge of possessiveness I'd expected.

Instead, the mark felt right. I ran my tongue over it, earning a shiver from my mate.

Pausing, I glanced up to take in her expression.

Fuck. So beautiful.

Her hair had turned silver with the power of the moon and her eyes were little moons burning with lust and magic.

Her skin swarmed with glittering power as if she lit up from within and everywhere I touched she *burned*.

Her heat would consume her if not tended to, but this would only help her along.

I kept my gaze on hers as I ran my tongue over her swollen nub, enjoying when she bucked in response.

"Hold her," I reminded Dash again.

His fingers dug into her hip and her breast, pressing little indents as he followed my lead.

It felt so fucking good to show my Goddess what I had been saving for her.

I drew her into my mouth.

And sucked as I thrust my fingers into her pussy.

She screamed as I worked my tongue and my mouth on her, building her pleasure until she was close to shattering.

The tension in the room was palpable. The other alphas had their full attention on our Goddess that was about to explode.

Shadow's gaze burned from behind and I wasn't sure how he was keeping himself in that chair.

Vern had knelt to one knee on the floor and watched in reverence and raw lust.

Dash held onto our Goddess, keeping her in place so that I could give her my full attention. I had no doubt she felt the pressure of his cock on her back.

Her body pulsed around my fingers when she hit her peak.

I sucked hard, rewarded when she *shattered*.

Ambrosia exploded over my tongue as she came and I kept going, working my mouth on her in time with her contractions.

I didn't stop until she went languid in Dash's arms.

"Very good, little wolf," Shadow praised with lust having a stranglehold on his voice. "Now tell us what you want."

KATLYN

Bliss.

   Pleasure.

   Ecstasy.

Ryker had made me come harder than I ever had in my life. Given recent experiences, that was saying something.

It wasn't just the level of his devotion or how he worshipped me with his tongue. It was also knowing I was being watched.

It was Dash's soft grip on me, occasionally wandering to my breast, my clit, or pressing into my hip to keep me in place.

His cock pressed against my back and the knowledge of his restraint honored me.

It was the thrill of how little I truly knew these alphas —but that excitement only drove me to new heights. Perhaps they had earned my trust, but they had yet to earn my heart.

If this was what it felt like to be worshipped by them, I wondered what it would feel like to be *loved* by them.

Because this was an arranged mating by the Goddess —by fate itself— and it was one where I would learn my mates and they would learn me.

Fate was a powerful force and I was tired of fighting it.

These were my allies against the true threat. The storms had taken my sister—*Althea* had taken her.

With the strength of my new mates, I would make her pay.

Dash watched from up close, occasionally skimming my shoulder with his teeth while Ryker licked me clean. My body trembled with each delicate stroke of his soft tongue.

Vern watched without moving. The pain on his face was evident. His muscles coiled from restraint.

He took in all of my pleasure as if it were oxygen itself, drawing in deep gulps of air as he panted.

Shadow wasn't faring much better. He'd crushed his glass in his grip and shards stuck in his flesh as blood trickled down the armrest of his chair.

He didn't seem bothered by it. Instead, he watched me and waited for my answer.

Because he'd just asked me what I wanted.

Ryker had denied my request to fuck me, but I knew it was more of a delay than a true denial.

He would fuck me, but he first wished to court me in his own way.

To *worship* me.

What I wanted was to have them join me in pleasure. I didn't wish for them to be in pain.

This was going to be a union of the packs that had yet to mark me.

It would not be a union made in pain.

But I couldn't accept all their knots. Biologically, I could only accept one at a time, and it would last for hours. By then, I would likely return to my body.

But there were other things I could have them do.

"I want you to touch yourself while you watch, Shadow," I said specifically to the Midnight Alpha.

If he truly meant to prove himself, then this was his test. I would only permit him the pleasure of his own hand and the sights before him.

At least for tonight.

Shadow's dark eyes flared with desire.

He methodically unbuttoned his pants, then pushed down the zipper, revealing his thick cock.

He wrapped his fingers around it and ran his thumb over the head, spreading the moisture of precum that had gathered there.

My tongue flashed out on my lower lip, wanting to taste.

Instead, I turned to Vern. He'd suffered exposure to the rains worse than the others, evident by the dark streaks of his veins, but he was still mine.

Still mine to command.

Still mine to protect.

The urge to protect the Valiance Alpha intrigued me, so that was the urge I decided to explore.

The wolf and Goddess inside of me provided a delightful image, one that made my body tighten with anticipation.

"On your back," I instructed Vern. "Naked."

My alphas seemed to enjoy this demanding side of me, but I was letting the Goddess lead me.

I had a feeling I would be rewarded for it.

Vern slowly peeled off his pants, revealing a deliciously beautiful cock that curved.

I wanted to feel that cock inside of me. It looked like it would touch all the right places. But, he was going to have to earn that privilege.

He reclined onto the bed on his back.

All of my alphas cursed when I straddled his face, then lowered my mouth onto his cock.

I'd done this position with a human before, but it felt different now.

I admired Vern's beautiful cock from up close as he took the invitation to kiss me from below. A shiver ran through my body as my temperature rose a notch.

If I burned much hotter, I felt like I might combust.

Thirst drove me to take Vern's cock down my throat. He groaned when the curve of it allowed me to take him deeper than I anticipated.

I sucked, then stroked, then licked, enjoying the control the position gave me.

I looked up at Ryker who knelt, rigid, waiting for my command.

"You're going to let me taste you before you fuck me. It's only fair," I said."

Ryker grinned, then must have decided not to wait any longer because he took off his pants.

And I stared.

Because he was pierced.

There.

A ring looped through his opening, making me salivate. I'd never seen any sort of accessory like that.

And the ring itself must have been made of some sort of special material, because it glowed with magic.

"Moon Silver," he explained as he stroked himself, then ran his finger over the piercing. "It's the only thing that'll remain in place for a wolf and not heal over."

I was glad he approached me, because I didn't have any words as I stared.

When he was close enough, I ran my tongue over him, enjoying his hiss of pleasure and the metallic taste of the ring.

Fuck, he was big. No wonder he had put so many fingers inside of me.

He competed with Shadow's length, and had the largest girth.

As much as I wanted to taste his cum, he was my chosen one to knot me tonight. I glanced up at him, knowing that neither of us had the restraint in place to stop.

Plus, I wanted to know what it felt like with that piercing inside of me.

But first, I had another alpha to tend to.

"Dash," I said, turning to him. I kept my hand firmly on Vern's cock, enjoying as it throbbed while he watched me take turns with the other alphas.

This was a union of the packs, one that now felt right to me. I wasn't forcing a mating, but instead letting my instincts guide me.

I licked my lips when Dash disrobed, revealing a thicker cock than all of the others.

Except for Ryker.

So, the alpha I had chosen for my blessing was the largest of them.

The Goddess inside of me practically giggled in response to my realization.

I tasted Dash, relishing his woodsy spice. I licked the lines of his abdomen, concentrating on tracing them with my tongue before finding myself drawn back to Vern's cock.

Vern was decadence and indulgence. The strong aromas of ginger and sage made me hum in delight as he worshipped my clit with his tongue.

Dash rested his head on Vern's chest, taking my breast into my mouth while Ryker's heat and sensual piercing pressed against my core from behind.

Ryker rubbed his thumb over me, preparing me, as he drew my wetness over my opening and my ass.

I didn't know why until I felt the pressure of his thumb.

I… liked it.

Glancing up, I found Shadow watching us as his jaw clenched. Raw heat bled from his dark eyes as he deliberately stroked himself, matching the strokes of Vern's tongue on my pussy.

Proving that he was watching every movement and caress.

Yes, he was earning his place in this pack.

Because I wasn't just uniting the packs. I was making a new one.

I ran my tongue over Vern's cock, enjoying the powerful notes of his taste before I spoke.

"Fuck me, Ryker. I won't order you again."

My command held a growl to it, one with power and magic that made all the alphas in the room respond.

Vern's cock gushed with precum and his teeth grazed my clit. The vibration of his growl felt so good, as did Dash's attention on my breast.

Dash was stroking himself and that pleased me as his pleasure joined the mixture of scents in the room.

He, too, was earning his place.

Pressure rewarded me from behind as Ryker slowly obeyed. The cool pleasure of his piercing added a sharp burst of sensual delight. He kept me in place simply by holding me with his thumb in my ass, making my eyes roll.

Vern continued his attention on my clit, seemingly unbothered by Ryker's closeness as the Mystic Alpha stretched me open with his cock and pressed that magical piercing further inside.

Pleasure splintered through my body as he continued, pushing me until I panted on Vern's cock. I held the base of it with both hands, attempting to take all of Ryker as I angled my hips.

He wouldn't be able to knot me until he was fully seated.

But damn if that wasn't a privilege *I* was the one to earn.

Vern lashed his tongue against me, making me tremble as Dash did the same. Their adoration made my body accept a little more of Ryker and he eased inside impossibly further.

I'd never felt so full in all my life.

"Almost there, little Goddess," Ryker told me.

I whimpered as my clit throbbed against Vern's attentions and my walls squeezed around Ryker. I moved, trying to momentarily get away from the pleasure so I could think straight, but Dash took on his role of keeping me in place. He reached up and held my arm as he lightly bit my nipple, punishing me for trying to move.

Shadow growled. "You're taking that cock like such a good girl," he praised, stroking himself harder. "He's going to fuck that pussy until he knots you, little wolf. Dash, Vern, and Ryker are all going to bite when you can't move. Then, you're going to come for us, aren't you?"

The image alone almost made me shatter.

Vern's heady taste made me feel drunk as I swallowed his cock, silencing my scream while Ryker pushed all the way to the hilt, softly slapping his hips against my ass.

Vern sucked on my clit, and Dash kept my nipple captive between his teeth.

Something broke inside of me, like a dam that was unleashed as wetness ran down my thighs.

My alphas growled in response, making me whimper and squirm against them, but I didn't want to get away this time.

I needed more. I needed Ryker to fill me and stretch me, give me all of his seed and his *bite*.

I demanded it by bouncing against him. Vern released my clit with a pop and held out his tongue, allowing me to graze my sensitive nub against it as I took his cock down my throat. My lungs burned for air, but I needed to chase this desire more than I needed to breathe.

Dash did the same, letting my nipple graze against his

sharp teeth as I slapped against Ryker's hips, matching his thrusts with ones of my own until we found a rhythm.

"That's it, little wolf," Shadow praised, driving me on. "Keep going. You're almost there."

Brilliant silver light overtook the room, blinding me as I heard Ryker growl.

It was a new sound, one that demanded my supplication and obedience.

I was a Goddess.

But I was also his Omega.

I spread my legs for him a little more, allowing him to take the lead as he drove into me, harder, faster, stroking every inch of me with his swollen cock. The sharp pleasure of his piercing only amplified my climb as I cried out.

My entire body slammed down on him, gripping him and milking him until he roared in response.

Pleasure blew through my body as his cock swelled inside of me, the base stretching me until that desperate need within me finally felt heard.

"He's knotting you, little wolf," Shadow said, making my pleasure even stronger with his praising voice. "You're the first pussy he's ever had. Milk him like a good girl."

He touched himself with hard, unforgiving strokes as he watched.

He'd promised me something after Ryker knotted me, hadn't he?

Sharp pleasure and pain radiated on my thigh when Vern sank his teeth into me.

I screamed as Dash bit next on the underside of my breast.

And finally Ryker leaned over me, stretching me from

the inside as he pulled me off of Vern's cock and licked my pulse.

"Come on my knot, little Goddess," he said, then sank his teeth into my neck.

The combination was too much.

I exploded, not just with pleasure, but with magic.

Waves of ecstasy rolled through my body as my heat finally broke on my scream. It lashed against me with unrelenting pulses and throbs.

Vern drew out the climax with his fingers, and Dash licked at the mark he had made, laving his tongue over my breast and nipple.

Shadow's come ran over his fingers as he watched me with sheer reverence.

When lucidity returned enough for me to realize why, I noticed the weight that had appeared on my head.

I reached up, finding a crown had materialized on my brow.

Shadow grinned.

"All hail the new Wolf Queen."

KANE

I jolted against the chains of my prison.

Dark chains made of Corruption, not Moon Magic.

Blinking at my surroundings, I took in the dim light of the cavern where I often kept prisoners. Althea wasn't here. Only the Goddess knew where she was or what she was up to.

But it didn't matter, because Kaitsja had won.

My vision was tinted in red as I allowed the bloodlust to consume me. It was the only thing keeping me separate from the Corruption tainting my mind, especially while my wolf was gone.

He had gone to fulfill my command.

One to coronate Kaitsja as Queen.

He must have succeeded, because I felt Her through our mate-bond unlike ever before.

Raw power.

Pure bliss.

Delight and *sex*.

"Good girl," I whispered, my voice ragged and broken, but proud of my Goddess.

She'd done what none had been able to do for generations.

She'd united the packs, earning Her the right to become the Wolf Queen.

Her coronation was complete, but She would need to be presented to the packs and receive their acceptance. That was the tricky part. A Goddess was only as strong as the faith of Her believers.

As much as I wished to honor Her with my worship, I was useless to Her like this.

My wolf's spirit appeared in the darkness, making me realize that's what had been providing light.

"You did it," I said, pleased with the wolf.

He stared at me with those moon orbs he had for eyes. I'd never separated my wolf's spirit from myself before. It was forbidden magic for our kind and left us vulnerable.

But desperate times called for desperate measures.

"Come back to me now," I told him, ready to feel complete again. I'd been hanging on by a thread since he'd been gone. My existence was nothing short of torture as I endured the violence of bloodlust and the chaos of Calamity's Corruption.

So much so that I didn't blame him when he lowered his head and growled.

"You're going to have me do this alone, hmm?" I asked. "Very well. Then kill me and be done with it, beast. Otherwise, I will succumb to this darkness soon enough."

I had no desire to be a threat to Kaitsja. Death was a much more suitable option.

My wolf snarled again, as if disgusted.

Fight, he seemed to say.

What did he think I'd been doing this whole time?

I had been fighting every moment, ensuring that Kaitsja took the wolf crown.

"It's no use, wolf. Every creature dies, even us."

I wasn't afraid of death.

What I truly feared was failing life.

And if this Corruption took my will from me and hurt my Goddess, then that was failure indeed.

My wolf snarled again and launched toward me.

I showed him my neck, ready for him to tear it out.

Instead, he sank his teeth into my chest and yanked.

A growl erupted from my throat as he pulled and tugged. Did the stupid beast get one of my ribs? What the hell was he doing?

A sharp pain speared through my heart and a clatter of metal sounded next.

I blinked and looked down, realizing that my wolf had just pulled something from my body.

He licked it, revealing what was underneath.

A rounded glimmer of silver left no guesses as to what he'd found.

The Moon King's crown.

"Take it to Her," I ground out.

It didn't surprise me that I had been the Moon King all along.

I would pass my crown onto another, if it meant Kaitsja would live.

My wolf whined and licked my wound. Moon Magic helped it to close.

"No, beast. Do as I say. Take the crown to Her and leave it to the Goddess to decide my fate."

My wolf and I didn't always agree with one another. But what we did have in common was our love for the Goddess.

With a blink of his intelligent eyes, he finally succumbed and scooped the crown into his sharp teeth.

Then he scampered away on a breeze of magic, leaving me alone in the darkness.

Where I would await my Goddess to hear my prayers.

Or Her condemnation.

That was my last thought before I succumbed to the penetrating chaos, and became what Althea intended me to be.

Darkness incarnate.

A broken Wolf King.

To be continued in Moon Kissed, the final book in the Crescent Five series!

Author's Note

Thank you for reading Moon Queen! This series has taken me on a wild ride and I couldn't be more thrilled to announce the continuation of Katlyn's story in Moon Kissed, the conclusion to the Crescent Five series!

There's still a lot of relationship development to unpack and I finally feel like all of the wolves are starting to talk to me. I was nervous there for the first two books because my wolves weren't as chatty as I'm used to when it comes to male romance leads.

Then Lyle was born.

This was an unintended character that changed everything for me and my love of this series. I went from struggling to thriving. My muse is a fickle creature and apparently she wasn't very happy that I had killed off Charlie. So she found a way to bring him back, and even better than before!

My wolves started talking to me once this shift occurred and I can't wait to let them shine in the final book of this series.

Reverse Harem Paranormal Romance - Never Choose.

J.R. Thorn is a Reverse Harem Paranormal Romance
Author who loves coffee, stormy weather, and heated
discussions with her inner muse. She can often be found
scribing her steamy stories in her writing cave far away
from the prying eyes of her toddler, husband, two vocal
cats, and canine pack!

www.AuthorJRThorn.com

facebook.com/BloodStoneSeries

FORTUNE ACADEMY: YEAR ONE SNEAK PEEK

Interested in reading Dante and Logan's Story? Be sure to check out Fortune Academy! Here is a sneak peek...

Fortune Academy: Chapter 1

It all started with a severed hand and a hot bounty hunter. For the record, I would never chop off the hand of a hot guy... unless he was being a total douchebag—which he was. Plus, it grew back, so it doesn't even really count... not that I was aware bounty hunters could regrow appendages, but hey, no harm no foul.

Right, I tend to blather on without context so let me start from the beginning, right around the time when my memories restarted in the middle of the street with no idea who I was. Boy, was I in for a surprise when I figured that one out.

The first thing I remember from that point on was my clothes sticking to my skin and my hair plastered to my cheeks from the freezing rain. Everything was sore as if I'd been run over by a bulldozer. I wandered, drawn by a pull that promised refuge until I found myself in a dark alley facing the back entrance of a bar. Raindrops hit my face like irritating little insects, but I couldn't seem to find the strength to leave this particular doorstep. Something bad had happened to me and I must have run until I couldn't run anymore. My legs trembled underneath me like jello and my heart wouldn't stop thundering in my ears. All I could do was gulp in breaths of air and wait for someone to open that dull, red door lined with scratches.

The moonlight was too bright, but I peered up at the sky and pleaded for mercy anyway. I didn't know what I needed mercy for, or why I was paralyzed in the freezing rain at this grimy doorstep, but I just knew that this was my last hope. I had to stay here until that door opened.

The streetlights blasted on and made me flinch, but I stared at the door until it opened and a woman in her late forties peered down at me with a disgusted scowl. She stared at me for a long time before she stepped aside. "Come on," she said, then turned around and left the entranceway free.

That's how I became Cindy's newest waitress. Waiting like a drowned rat at the back of her bar to what was supposed to be her secret entrance reserved for smoke breaks. Well, that's how all supernaturals found Cindy. Now when I walked outside I could spot the little ugly engraving in the corner of the doorway that drew people like me to the place. A little tiny skull etched there with a dumb grin on its face like it knew how many headaches it would bring Cindy. This was her punishment... to help people like me who had no memory of who they were or what they'd done. Ever since the Second Echo of Calamity apparently the world had gone to all sorts of shit and supernaturals had to start over with clean slates, memories included. What Cindy had done to deserve her fostering of looney supernaturals, I had no idea and she wasn't about to admit it to me.

The thing was, Cindy attracted just that, supernaturals. Sure, something was off about me, but even I felt like I didn't quite fit in with the supernatural crowd of misfits. I had a feeling that my memory loss didn't have much to do with the whacky weirdness that was going on with the world. It was something more personal... but Cindy didn't have to know that.

I liked Cindy. She never asked questions or gave me a hard time when I didn't seem to know basic things. It felt like I had to learn how to live life all over again. Something fundamental had changed in me and I couldn't put my finger on what. Without having any memory of my past, I wasn't even going to try and figure it out. Let it come naturally, that's what Cindy always said.

We had this weird kind of understanding that made our relationship work. I'd shown up on her doorstep in the middle of the night covered in blood and soaked with rain and she'd taken me in just like she'd done with so many before me.

That's what the mother of monsters always did.

"Guy at table three has been ogling you for an hour," Jess told me as she balanced a tray on her hip.

Jess was the closest thing I had to a friend in the same way that Cindy was the closest thing I had to a mother. Jess had arrived only a few weeks before I did, but she was already well on her way to recovery. Cindy had set up a few interviews for Jess at various escort gigs. Normally I'd disapprove, but Jess seemed to love the attention, so I hoped she would be happy when it was time for her to go.

"Don't be a bimbo," I said, making a point to ignore the guy she'd pointed out. "No way he's looking at me when you're standing right here." I gave her short skirt and halter top a raised brow. She already had voluptuous boobs and a rounded ass big enough to make a guy stop in his tracks, and that outfit made everything pop in just the right way. "I'm not a succubus like you."

She grinned, showing off her pearly white teeth. "I'm serious, Lily, he's checking you out!"

Dread washed over me. I had the good looks, sure. Long, blonde hair, legs that could kill in some heels and plump lips that would be perfect for pouting... if I ever pouted, which I didn't. I desperately hoped that I wasn't a succubus.

I still didn't know what I was yet, which was frustrating, but since being a succubus was still on the table I scanned the bar just for good measure. Every guy in the place was drooling over Jess and making a fool of themselves... every guy except for the one at table three.

Our gazes matched long enough for a jolt of familiar awareness to slam through me.

Okay, that was weird.

I tried to pretend I was fascinated with my phone. "I'm off duty, Jess," I reminded her as I scrolled through a mindless social media thread. "Go give the guy a new beer. The one you gave him an hour ago looks flat and he's probably just thirsty."

"Yeah," she snickered and waggled her eyebrows, "thirsty for some of your lo-ove," she said, making sure to sing-song the last word.

Ignoring her, I continued to scroll through my phone. It wasn't hard to pretend my fascination when the damn thing was so addictive. Cindy allowed me to use it as long as it was only for "research," as she called it. I never called anyone or posted anything online. I loved to read about humans and see what kinds of things they shared with each other. Most of it involved vague statements I didn't understand, pictures of kittens—which I always approved of—and snaps of perfectly arranged meals. Then there was the occasional political post about the emergence of supernaturals. Everyone had an opinion, especially when it came to Fortune Academy. *A Place Where Supernaturals Belong.* That was their slogan.

When I'd asked Cindy about it, she'd sneered and told me that if I was smart, I'd steer clear of anything related to that place.

Not that I was going to tell Cindy my opinion, but she had to be wrong. An entire organization dedicated to helping lost supernaturals? While I appreciated all that Cindy did for me, she didn't have answers. Fortune Academy would give me a fighting chance at figuring out what the hell I was.

One slight problem… the academy had stringent perquisites to join, one of which is demonstrating a supernatural ability—which I hadn't been able to do yet. I only knew I was supernatural because I'd lost my memories and Cindy's door rune had called me to her.

I'd figure out what I was… but it wasn't going to be easy.

Jess elbowed me in the ribs. "Hey, are you listening to me?"

I rolled my eyes. "You're still here? I said I was busy."

She leaned in and lowered her voice, not taking her eyes off the stranger. "I really think you should go talk to him, Lils. I can tell when a guy has the hots, and while he definitely has the hots for you, something is off about him that I can't really figure out. I don't like it."

I chuckled. "I'll tell you what's off about him. There's a gorgeous succubus in the room and he's staring at me. Clearly the guy's missing some marbles." And of course she didn't like it. Jess needed to get all of the male attention—which was fine with me.

"Hey, sweet cheeks!" A guy from across the bar yelled at Jess. "You bringing me those beers, or what?"

Jess waved at him and giggled, which just pissed me off. "You should go kick that guy in the balls."

Jess huffed and readjusted her tray. "That's not how I get the good tips. Now go talk to the hottie at table three or I will." She pursed her lips and gave me a you-better-go-talk-to-him-or-else look and then marched over to deliver the impatient human his beers.

I turned my attention back to the topic of our discussion. The stranger hunched into himself, hiding his face in the shadow of his cowl. I frowned.

That either meant he was shy, or he was hiding something.

Someone who could resist a succubus' charms wasn't the shy type, so I stuffed my phone in the back of my jeans pocket and marched over to his table. I crossed my arms until he grunted at me.

"Oh, so you can talk?" I snapped. Irritation put me on edge. I was standing right in front of him and he wouldn't look up at me. "What, you can stare at me all night when I'm halfway across the room but when I come to your table you've got nothing to say?"

He twisted the untouched beer that Jess had delivered to him an hour ago, leaving a ring of condensation on the table. "So, you don't remember me." His voice came out husky and low… and apparently he knew who I was.

My entire body froze and a cold sweat broke out on my face. I'd harbored the secret hope that someone might recognize me in a popular bar, but I'd also feared the day someone who knew me might show up. I'd arrived at a monster's orphanage… and I'd been soaked in more than icy rain that night I'd shown up at Cindy's doorstep.

Yes I'd been covered in blood—but it was blood that wasn't my own. By the time I got my clothes off that night and slipped into a borrowed set of pajamas, I discovered I didn't have a single scratch on me.

I somehow managed to swallow the bitter fear that crawled up my throat. Letting out a nervous laugh, I flipped my hair over my shoulder. Guys always reacted better when they thought I was a dumb blonde. "Sorry. Maybe if you weren't hiding behind your cowl I could actually see your face, you know? Hard to jostle the memory with just a broody voice."

He hesitated and then shifted so that his cowl moved just enough for me to see the hard ridge of his chin. "I don't brood," he growled.

It was almost cute how he immediately retorted the insult. I was about to make it worse, but then he pulled back his hood all the way and hot damn, the guy was smoking.

And, well, his eyes glowed with a metallic orange magic that marked him as a supernatural bounty hunter... but yeah, details.

I shouldn't have been surprised that a bounty hunter would show up at Cindy's bar, but he still managed to take me off guard. While my mind was mush, my body reacted to the deadly flash of silver that was his blade. The world around me stilled with a magical lock. I didn't know if it was something I'd done or if it had been the bar's defenses. Taking advantage of the moment, I twisted to put as much distance as possible between me and the hunter.

Except... he tracked my movements with ease, his eyes locked onto mine as I moved. When I flinched, he flicked the blade and its merciless silver etched across my vision. I knew it would be sharp enough to cut my head clean off my body, but I realized a half-second too late that he hadn't been aiming for me.

Jess cried out and clutched at the embedded hilt,

crumpling to the floor as time unlocked from its slowed momentum.

"Jess!" I screamed and lurched to her aid, but the hunter had me by the arm with a vice grip.

"You're welcome," he growled and tugged me into his chest. "She was about to kill you."

Flattened against his hard abs, I curled my fingers into the thick layers of his coat and peered up at him, taking in the full brutal force of his hard edges and glowing eyes. Everything about him screamed danger, but the way he held me was protective... almost gentle.

A clatter of metal hit the floor and broke a silence that I realize didn't make any sense in a crowded bar. No one seemed to notice that Jess had been stabbed, or that a hunter with glowing eyes was holding me.

That was because time was frozen... but not Jess.

Jess... who now had a dagger plunged in her chest.

Even a succubus should have died from a mortal wound like that, but she snarled as if irritated by the blade and launched for me. The hunter reacted before I did and held out his hand to defend me, which would have been sweet, except the weapon struck clean through flesh and bone, severing his hand and sending it flopping to the floor like a lump of meat.

"Oh dear..." I murmured.

He cursed and wrapped the stumped remains of his hand in his cloak. When Jess cried out and collapsed to her knees, I realized that he hadn't cursed under his breath, but rather cast a spell.

So, my bounty hunter had some magical mojo.

"You bastard!" Jess screamed. "She's mine!"

My brain couldn't process Jess screaming at the hunter, so my gaze wandered throughout the bar that was like a snapshot in time.

A group three tables down held up their beers in celebration and one sloshed his contents into the air, the foam and droplets making a perfect arc over his friend's head.

Cars outside that should have been speeding down the dark alleyway were now stopped. The one closest to the window featured a woman with her hair fanned out behind her as if she was trapped in a photoshoot.

Then I spotted Cindy watching from the back with the door cracked open. Even she was trapped in the moment. Whatever had frozen time, only the hunter, Jess, and I were able to move. It bothered me more that Cindy was just back there... watching... as if waiting for something to happen. If she knew who the hunter was, why wouldn't she have stopped me from talking to him?

The hunter shook me with his remaining hand. He should have been buckled over in pain, but I didn't know much about bounty hunters. Maybe he could shut his pain off. "You need to stop daydreaming," he snapped. "Look." He pointed and my gaze obeyed even though my brain didn't want to process what was going on.

A knife rested on the ground just inches from Jess's hand, but not the one the hunter had stabbed her with. That one was still lodged in her chest and blood pooled around the wound and seeped into her clothing.

"Jess?" I asked, my voice cracking when I finally realized that she'd been coming at us with a knife. Not just any knife, but a blade etched with runes that glowed red.

I considered Jess my friend, even though I'd only been here a few weeks and was still trying to remember who I was. Cindy told me that I shouldn't rush it. Just take as much time as I needed. Jess had always been supportive in her own way, but this wasn't the Jess who talked to me about guys or stole a shot with me from behind the bar. She gripped the hilt of the dagger still embedded in her chest and glared at me. I'd never seen anyone look at me with such hatred, much less someone I thought was my friend.

"You're a monster," she said, almost like it was something she'd kept in for far too long. "You're supposed to work for us. No one else can have you!" She lurched for the dagger she'd dropped, but cried out in pain and slapped her hand on the floor.

If it hadn't been for the hunter who still held me with one strong arm, I would have gone ice cold. I hadn't been in many situations where I was this stressed, but sometimes when a customer got rowdy or Cindy raised her voice my fingertips would go so cold that they'd feel numb until I grabbed onto someone. Now the urge to touch devoured me worse than I'd ever felt it and I crawled my hands up the hunter's clothes until I reached a patch of skin exposed at his neck. He flinched the moment my icy fingers met his, but he didn't stop me. Instead he stroked my hair out of my eyes and gave me a sobering look.

"It's Lily, right?"

Hearing my name jolted me into awareness and I looked into his eyes that still glowed with that fascinating metallic golden gleam. "Uh, yeah." How did he know my name?

He surveyed the bar and frowned. "I can't hold the time lock once we step outside of this bar. We're lucky that the monster mother was on the other side of the door when I initiated it." He glanced down at the dagger still in Jess's chest. I noticed one gem on the end of the hilt glowing green, but that light was starting to fade. "We don't have much longer. Do you think you can move?"

The shock of what he was proposing made all the heat I'd gathered into my fingertips surge straight through my whole body. He jerked away from me and cursed.

"You can't mean that I'd go somewhere with you?" I asked.

"Yes," he growled, transforming from the kind and patient stranger I'd been clinging to back into the hunter that had come to... what had he come here to do? "If you stay here you'll be killed... or worse. You have to come with me."

Sense came back to me as I bristled. No one told me what to do. "I can take care of myself, thank you very much."

"You better listen to him," Jess drawled, grinning manically as her eyelids drooped and blood tinted her teeth pink. It was the most terrifying sight I'd ever seen, especially since one side of her face was starting to droop and one of her eyes was turning black. "I'm not really a succubus, you know. I'm something else... something even better. I wasn't ready to show you, but looks like I don't have a choice. You lost your memory because you weren't ready to learn what you are, but I've embraced it."

"You shut your mouth," the hunter snapped and produced a second blade. "Lily is nothing like you."

She gurgled on another laugh. "Oh, protective, are you? Didn't come to kill her... but to collect her for your little academy? How quaint."

I dug my fingernails into my palm. The air around us started to tremble as if the whole world was about to fall apart. I couldn't leave Jess here, dying, even if she was frightening me. I didn't care what she was, I needed to give her a chance to explain. Maybe if she thought I wouldn't go with him she'd stop trying to attack me.

She gave me a look of pity. Which was incredulous. Jess, the one with the knife in her chest and her face falling apart, gave *me* a look of pity. "Such a sweet thing. You still want to help me, don't you?" She sighed. "Tricky blood you have. Two-thirds of you is perfect for Monster Academy, but there's that nasty little extra third that shows its ugly head. I see it right now in your eyes. No proper monster would look at me like that." Her face twisted with rage. "Mother will burn it out of you. Then you can join us and Monster Academy will finally have its star pupil." She chuckled. "Or failed experiment. Either way, I will be getting some major extra credit for this."

"Monster Academy?" I shrieked. "Jess, what the hell are you talking about?"

She opened her mouth to answer me, but a loud crack reverberated through the room and time unlocked from its latch.

"Time to go," the hunter said and took me by the arm again.

Everything happened all at once. The serene silence

dropped into a clatter of noise typical of a busy bar. Startled, I ducked as if the bombardment of sounds was an object hurled at my head, and good thing, too. Cindy burst through the door and launched fire—fucking fire!—from her hand.

I'd never seen anything like it. The flames were so hot that they melted straight through a pair of guests and sent their corpses disintegrating to the floorboards. The bar exploded and the scent of fear hit me like a wall.

"Come on!" the hunter shouted and tugged at me, but I was rooted to the spot. He gave me a look of surprise.

That's right. I was supernatural. No fucking idea what I was, but he wasn't going to move me unless I agreed to it.

Which, going with him was starting to feel like a good idea. Jess was talking about hooking me up with Monster Academy—no idea what that was but it didn't sound good—and Cindy was throwing fire around and killing people.

I had a decision to make and not much time to make it. One quick glance at Jess gave me mixed feelings. She clearly wasn't a succubus. Jess's beauty melted off of her as if the dagger in her chest drained her of her outer skin. I wasn't sure if it had been a spell or some elaborate magical sleeve, but whatever this creature was before me now with black eyes and wrinkled skin was the real Jess.

Strangely, I wanted to get to know her. Those black eyes still had Jess inside of them. There was more darkness and pain, but still the friend that I'd come to care for.

Yet, when she went for the cool blade again on the floor, I knew that she would rather kill me than let the hunter have me. Perhaps I was naive, just like she always told me I was.

Closing my eyes with resignation, I let the hunter haul me out of the bar and into the cold night.

Of course, it was fucking raining, and the blood on me wasn't my own.

Keep Reading Fortune Academy on Amazon

RECOMMENDED READING ORDER

All Books are Standalone Series listed by their sequential order of events

Elemental Fae Universe Reading List

- Elemental Fae Academy: Books 1-3 (Co-Authored)
- Midnight Fae Academy (Lexi C. Foss)
- Fortune Fae Academy (J.R. Thorn)
- Fortune Fae M/M Steamy Episodes (J.R. Thorn)
- Candela (J.R. Thorn)
- Winter Fae Queen (Co-Authored)
- Hell Fae (Co-Authored)

Blood Stone Series Universe Reading List
Recommended Reading Order is Below

Seven Sins
- *Book 1: Succubus Sins*

- *Book 2: Siren Sins*

- *Book 3: Vampire Sins*

The Vampire Curse: Royal Covens

- *Book 1: Her Vampire Mentors*

- *Book 2: Her Vampire Mentors*

- *Book 3: Her Vampire Mentors*

Fortune Academy (Part I)

- *Year One*

- *Year Two*

- *Year Three*

Fortune Academy Underworld (Part II)

- *Episode 1: Burn in Hell*

- *Book Four*

- *Episode 2: Burn in Rage*

- *Book Five*

- *Book Six*

- *Episode 3: Burn in Brilliance*

Fortune Academy Underworld (Part III)

- *Book Seven*

- *Book Eight*

- *Book Nine*

- *Book Ten*

Crescent Five *(Rejected Mate Wolf Shifter RH)*

- *Book One: Moon Guardian*

- *Book Two: Moon Cursed*

- *Book Three: Moon Queen*

- *Book Four: Moon Kissed*

Dark Arts Academy (Vella)

Ongoing serial

- *Book One (KU)*

- *Book Two (KU)*

Unicorn Shifter Academy

- *Book One*

- *Book Two*

- *Book Three*

Non-RH Books (J.R. Thorn writing as Jennifer Thorn)

Noir Reformatory Universe Reading List

Noir Reformatory: The Beginning (Standalone)

Noir Reformatory: First Offense

Noir Reformatory: Second Offense

Noir Reformatory Turns RH from this point with the addition of a third mate

Noir Reformatory: Third Offense

Sins of the Fae King Universe Reading List

(Book 1) Captured by the Fae King

(Book 2) Betrayed by the Fae King

Learn More at www.AuthorJRThorn.com

Made in the USA
Monee, IL
17 October 2023

44707429R00187